Waiting *for* Rescue

A NOVEL

Lucy Honig

COUNTERPOINT
BERKELEY

The author thanks The Writers' Room of Boston, The Blue Mountain Center, and
Hall Farm Center for providing shelters in which this book was hatched. Very special
gratitude to agent Emilie Jacobson and editor Roxanna Aliaga.

Pages from the novel in somewhat altered form were published as the short story
"A Research Project" in *Peregrine,* Volume XXV, 2008.

Library of Congress Cataloging-in-Publication Data

Honig, Lucy, 1948–
Waiting for rescue : a novel / Lucy Honig.
p. cm.
ISBN 978-1-58243-527-5
1. September 11 Terrorist Attacks, 2001—Psychological aspects—Fiction.
2. Psychological fiction. I. Title.

PS3558.O53W35 2009
813'.54—dc22

2009019256

Cover design by Ann Weinstock
Interior design by Megan Jones Design
Printed in the United States of America

COUNTERPOINT
2117 Fourth Street
Suite D
Berkeley, CA 94710

www.counterpointpress.com

Distributed by Publishers Group West

10 9 8 7 6 5 4 3 2 1

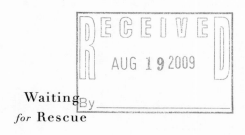

Waiting
for Rescue

To the memory of

Galgallo, Ruta, Carmen, Mohamed, Keisha, and Nthabi

Waiting
for Rescue

One

❖

It begins, midway, with a simple scene. A quick take.

THEY'D SET UP camp with bundles and coats and prayer rugs at
the end of the hallway, beside the immense windows that rose to
the ceiling. None of the nurses had the heart to stop them; nobody
could have possibly imagined how long it would all go on. Six flights
below, Boston honked and squawked and blared its way through a
rainy rush-hour gridlock, but up here, the length of the hall, a thick
hush prevailed. Pausing at the doorway of Ibrahim's room, I saw
only the pulled curtain and knew he was being examined or washed
or bandaged or relieved of excretions too indelicate for even his
own family to see. I continued toward the encampment. His mother
and father, who had arrived just a few days before from Khartoum,
stood at the big, drizzle-wormed window, looking down at par-
allel lines of headlights and taillights, mesmerized by the glowing
streams. His sister sat doing needlework. Ibrahim's mother, draped
in orange, gold, and green patterned cloths, shivered and drew her
shawled *hijab* more tightly around her shoulders. Her husband held
Ibrahim's youngest son, the impish toddler, who gave a silent kick
to reclaim for himself his grandfather's wandering attention. The
grizzled old man squeezed Karim in a hug, then slowly lowered

himself onto the floor cross-legged with the boy in his lap. Without a word, he pulled an orange from the big brown grocery bag, now half empty, that I had brought the day before. Karim watched, enrapt. The old man slowly peeled the orange, lifting the skin away in one ragged piece. He loosened the sections of fruit so they fanned out from the center, the whole still intact. Then gently he pulled off one section and put it in his own mouth. His eyes lit up with laughter as he put another plump orange morsel between Karim's surprised but eager lips.

Two

❖

Her work started to have that edginess, that grating, catchy, ultramodern, postmodern, a-little-discomfiting but not-too-discomfiting push and pull to it. But what is edgy anyway? She didn't know. She didn't even care. She used the word, but what did it mean? What did it have to do with her?

OR ANYBODY. I wasn't there, in lower Manhattan. Years ago I was always there. That was where my younger life was, and that's the place I still associate with life. With youth. Possibility. Unending possibility. But not for many years now has my own life been there, young and full of unending possibility. I didn't know anyone who died there that day either. I saw it on TV starting right after the first plane hit. Toby, who got to work early like I did, came to my office saying a plane had just slammed into the World Trade Center. Quickly we turned on the TV. No, I'm getting mixed up, Toby already had the radio on. Now I remember: at first it was radio, we listened to a radio in an office I didn't go into much, the turf of the research program staff. (Now I call it *the harem* because it's all young women, now it's only bright and thin young women in these jobs, in these unprivate spaces, with their short skirts and body piercings, their diamond engagement rings and fragile expectations.) On the radio I heard that the second tower was hit. Not long after, I heard about the Pentagon. I heard about other planes that had bolted from their radar-tracked paths, rerouted for destruction. Listening to the radio, I braced myself for the end of the world, as if I had been through it once before. First there would be power failures, I knew. Massive blackouts. Planes crashing into buildings everywhere. Conflagration. Unimaginable mayhem. Like nightmares I'd already had.

And full frontal defense talk. Old military men were already saying it when we finally rolled the TV into a conference room and other colleagues began to take seats and watch reruns of the planes flying into the towers for the umpteenth time, the TV forcing the day back over and over again to an endless 8:46. This is nothing like anything we've ever known before, barked the talking heads. Already, even before the towers crumbled, the old soldiers who had been biding their time were saying we would have to trade off some freedom to be safe. Surrender freedom to defend freedom. Attack someone to defend someone. Sure. Even then, I said, Oh sure, isn't this just *their* perfect opportunity? It couldn't have worked out better if they'd planned it all themselves.

IT WAS TOBY who told me first, Toby who had the radio on and then the TV. Toby who soon after switched to the Resource Impacts portfolio and got a promotion. Toby then moved out of what became, once he was gone, the harem. None of the women just as smart as he was did. And most of them were just as smart as he was, if not smarter. This is a university department, with more and more research bringing in government bucks, teaching pushed further and further to the frilly hems and cuffs. (Because all I do is teach, day by day at this place I sink deeper into my own unfunded irrelevance.) They did the degrees, these women so much younger than me, they were ripe for research, but they were stuck here in the dead dead-end. Now Toby has his own office, his own window, and four real walls. Now Toby's wife just had a baby. That's what they do, these young men in these times of fast unraveling. They get their promotions, they leave the smart women of the cubicles in the dust, they have their private little offices, their cute little families, the smart wives who have *their* degrees, too, but say they like staying home, and they become modern dads who wheel the babies around the park, sometimes every day, the good sports giving the women a break, the dads shouting work to each other on their cell phones in the parks. What will become of these kids whose fathers forget them in their carriages and strollers while they're shouting on the phone?

Now Toby makes his career coordinating some of our department's research studies; he is not the principal investigator of any, he is not an investigator at all, but he is the glue, as they say, that holds them all together. First he was on the Botswana study, which determined how much profit the mining companies lose when their workers get AIDS and miss work. (Not much, it turned out. They can dump the sick ones and hire new ones—the not-yet-half-dead ones already lined up at the gate desperate for a job, any job—and incur virtually no additional expenses.) Now he's got the Nairobi project. What happens when families who are already skittering off the edge of destitution have to take in the nieces and nephews and grandchildren and cousins whose parents die of AIDS? How do those families fare? For a million tax dollars, they'll find out. As if we didn't already know.

Poor Toby. What did he ever do to me? Nothing. But he's taken up with the wrong crowd.

FIRST WE SAW the figure 50,000. Fifty thousand people would be working in those buildings. Who was so angry, so hateful, so indifferent to fifty thousand lives? My first thought was the ones right here: the CIA, the FBI, the Christian fundamentalists, the men who did the thinking for the president. And the angry old men who had lost Viet Nam. I didn't think of other terrorists at first; I didn't think of other fundamentalists. Shame on me. Fifty thousand people would be working in those buildings. Thousands more were passing through, underneath, on and off the trains. I knew those people. For a while long ago, living in TriBeCa and doing the adjunct instructor's juggling act, I took PATH trains to and from Newark for a teaching gig. Underneath the twin towers, on my way from sweltering Newark to an overly air-conditioned night job teaching Spanish-speaking workers at a downtown leather handbag factory, I once got a frozen yogurt. Chocolate. In a sugar cone. Between gigs, I stood paralyzed for a minute or two in my daily weather-free underground miasma with a bolt of ice-cream pain holding my temples hostage. Brain freeze. Waiting for the throbs to subside, I watched that revved-up helter-skelter city underneath the towers, its frenetic momentum right then driven by nothing more, it seemed, than its own frenetic momentum. It was at that moment, motionless, clinging to my melting, half-eaten yogurt cone as the cold drilled through my skull, witnessing New York chase its own tail, I decided to leave the city. The city above. The city below. I decided to leave the city and to leave my husband of twelve years. The frenetic city down below also would have died that day. Maybe one hundred thousand people would be dead altogether. Maybe even more. In the conference room with all the others, I watched the TV in silence. I got ready for the end. Soon it would be us, too, here in this buttoned-down make-believe city where the first two planes took off. It was just a matter of time.

IVAN HAD COME to the office straight from a meeting on the other side of campus, and somehow he hadn't yet heard. He was always the sensitive one, the one in whom even the world's smallest misfortunes reverberated; he would take it badly. I ran into him in the hallway at 10:45. The short end of his funny flying-stethoscopes tie was caught inside his shirt, between the buttons; I resisted the impulse to yank it out. The tie was a vestige of his days as a practicing doctor, but he hadn't had the heart to deal with sick and dying people in the flesh, so he'd become a social epidemiologist, dealing instead with morbidity and mortality on the page. Not that he shirks. Oh no, Ivan's no shirker. His world-renown specialty is inequity between groups, economic disparities in care and well-being. A worthy focus, of course, if we must prove over and over and over again (which it seems we must) that people squeezed in the vise of misery are more likely to suffer poor health.

With tousled salt-and-pepper hair, blacker where it curled over his collar, Ivan always appeared endearingly disheveled, even when everything was where it should be, as it usually was. But that tie half in, half out meant something was already wrong, as if the planet itself were now askew.

I did not want to be the one who told anyone, but I had to tell Ivan. His face shattered like an old china plate. "Oh no, Erika, no," he rasped. Tears appeared instantly and spilled onto his cheeks. I hugged him. He was so tall and so solid, but he clung to me for a moment, as if he had lost his balance. "Was everybody killed?"

"Nobody knows yet," I said. "Nobody knows."

THE WORLD'S END ambushes you at school. It happened long before, too, in biology class, with Mr. Edwards. Mr. Edwards. A nice unobtrusive American name, a first name or a last name, except for the final *s*, it goes either way. Edward. Edwards. He was right out of teachers' college, taking his baby steps on us during that humbling first year in his own classroom. Don't wince. We were easy kids in the upstate backwaters, we broke him in gently. We did not have attitude, we did not have edge back then. He was a smudgy, lumpy dumpling of a guy, nice but utterly forgettable. And round: round-shouldered with a round stomach and a round doughy face with features still not quite set, he was an unbaked cinnamon bun of a man. Young. Undistinguished. An annoying Dennis-the-Menace cowlick sprouted from his too-far left-side part.

I was in biology class, first row right, and round Mr. Edwards was talking about amphibians up front, center left, when the door opened, far right. Hank Tully stuck his head in. Hank Tully was a junior, a prankster, always joking. But this was not his class. He looked all discombobbled. Rumpled. Streak-faced. What kind of joke was he playing now?

"Kennedy's been shot. They shot Kennedy in Dallas." That's what Hank Tully said. Right away we knew he wasn't joking. He

10

disappeared as quickly as he'd arrived, letting the door close with a soft thud.

Stunned, we all just sat there. Mr. Edwards who was supposed to be the grown-up sank down on his stool and sat there, too. We all watched him, waiting for a responsible adult to fix this mess, but Mr. Edwards didn't fix it. Eventually, though, he must have said something; eventually the class must have finished. I don't remember what he said or what we did then. But it's a cliché now, you always remember where you were when you heard Kennedy was shot. A part of you is stuck forever in that stunned silence of Mr. Edwards's science room after Hank Tully told you Kennedy was shot and shut the door as unexpectedly as he'd just opened it, moving quickly on to other classrooms, to other kids who would for a split second think he was pulling one of his dumb jokes again and then know right away in their gut of guts that this was not a joke.

Not when it happened but when you heard: that's what you remember. The next day we all saw Ruby shoot Oswald in real time on TV. We saw it for ourselves at the exact same time we heard.

By this time nearly everyone was in the conference room, watching television. So we saw the first tower go, slipping down further and further into its roaring guts, vanishing into the gigantic dust cloud composed of what just a few seconds before had been steel and concrete and glass and thousands of people who'd gone to work that ordinary Tuesday morning just like I had.

"Holy shit." Toby was the first one to say it. And then he giggled.

The second tower went down.

11

"Holy shit," said Toby again.

Fifty thousand people. It couldn't be. Others were on the street coated with that ghostly dust, fleeing for their lives.

"My God!" Toby laughed outright. We pretended not to notice his laughter. We were all now in some way unhinged, too.

The Pentagon, the field in Pennsylvania. What was next? All planes were called in out of the sky. But I knew buildings would fall like dominos across the vast land. Martial law would be imposed. Maybe some of us would be left. But for what?

"HOLY SHIT," I said. I had already read most of the article, the sordid story. The distinguished if quirky professor and amiable family man, father of two little girls and a boy, had chopped up a prostitute and strewn pieces of her in Dumpsters along the New Jersey Turnpike, pieces that were never found. To buy her gifts, he'd been embezzling from his grants. He was on some cutting edge of this or that, way before the genome or stem cell days; his grants were huge. Some speculated that certain parts of the very pretty girl went down the incinerator chutes at his lab. How the newspapers love it when a genius falls (though of course they love it even more when it's a rock star or politician). I was in TriBeCa, in my hectic twilight of unending possibility, reading the very long article in the *Village Voice*.

"Holy shit! That's my high school biology teacher!"

It had been more than twenty years, biology class long forgotten except for the opening and closing of the door, Hank Tully's tear-streaked face. Kennedy's been shot. I had never known a murderer before, but this Professor Edwards, this convict Edwards, this Edwards whose passions drove him to embezzle, deceive, buy lavish gifts, betray his family, and kill, this guy was *my* Mr. Edwards. I read the tabloids that covered the trial and plowed through the trashy books that followed; I saw the sleazy made-for-TV movie. I tried to imagine the twists by which a forgettable dumpling became a distinguished professor (already a stretch), a desperate lover and embezzler, a hulking monster taking the ax from his suburban garden shed to the human flesh he'd so adored. My brain couldn't handle it. I forgot him again.

I SAT WITH Ivan, my colleague of the flying stethoscopes tie. We were side by side on the crumbling stone steps leading down from the seawall, right across the street from my house. We had never done this before, though we had worked together for years. He has a girlfriend with a job somewhere in Central Asia. I am long divorced but have strident inner voices nay-saying workplace romance. But this was different. This was not romance. This was the world coming to an end, and we were the only ones who still seemed to be upset two days after the attacks. Ivan set the wine bottle on a step. We sipped from our glasses. Barely a ripple disturbed the water; we could see clearly to the bottom, the rounded stones and silt and mussel shells and strands of seaweed and worn-down shards of green bottle glass visible even at high tide. A glistening school of tiny fish swam by, in no particular hurry. A lone seagull cried out; smaller shorebirds twittered and peeped. Across the bay in the soft glow of the late afternoon sun, the Boston skyline sparkled in all its incoherence.

"It doesn't pass muster as a skyline," I said.

"You really are a New Yorker at heart, aren't you?"

"And you a Leningradite? A St. Petersbourger?"

"I left there too young. I belong nowhere. I am an -ite of nothing, I'm an -er of nowhere."

I leaned my shoulder against his. "A nowherite. A nothinger. Maybe it's just as well."

He grimaced. "With every named place in the world as screwed up as it is . . ." Ivan would have thrived in a mythical Soviet life for which he is sometimes still nostalgic; the capitalist triumphs left him high and dry and sad.

I sat up straight again and gestured out in front of us, to the skyline across Dorchester Bay. "I am not convinced by this scattering of skyscrapers that we have a city here. A *real* city."

"Of course Boston's a city. It thinks it's a city, so it has to be a city." Ivan was big on self-definition.

"But except for that cluster of sort-of skyscrapers downtown, the financial district, where the money grows very tall in buildings side by side"—I pointed more pointedly—"now *that* piece has credibility as a skyline—but the rest? Ugh. The Prudential building here, the Hancock over there, the random office towers, each one so isolated and vulnerable."

"*Now* you think 'vulnerable.'"

"Yeah. But I never liked it, even before this."

"But Erika, you didn't worry, 'somebody is going to crash and knock that down.'"

I thought for half a minute. "No, I did not worry about that before Tuesday."

We sat and looked and sipped. It was eerily quiet: where usually I watched the flight path of carefully spaced, traffic-controlled airplanes coming in to land, this day there was nothing. The day before there was nothing. Only the mocking blue sky without a cloud and without a contrail, the gentle lapping of waves, which pretended it was still summer, the illusion that life went lazily on. Nature told us all was right with the world and made a mockery of our dread and grief.

"These last two mornings, the first thing I did when I woke up was check to make sure all those stupid buildings were still there. No more gaping holes than usual. No architectural decapitations. No clouds of black smoke."

As we kept sitting, our silence was broken by the buzz of a Coast Guard boat patrolling the inner harbor. Then a single, louder drone followed a military plane which looped over the outer harbor, crisscrossed above the airport. The air force jets had been the only craft up there since Tuesday.

After a while Ivan said, "This would be the perfect vantage point to see Boston get blown up."

The buzz of the patrol boat and drone of the air force plane subsided. Quiet reigned again, a quiet that could almost pass for serenity. He put an arm around my shoulders, squeezed in an awkward hug as we still both faced out to the sea and skyline, and then drew the arm back to himself.

"Look, the cruise ships." I pointed to the partly visible extremities of docked vessels that had turned back or been diverted from New York. With my cheap binoculars, we could make out the huge smokestacks, the tiered decks, a temporary shantytown of gigantic steel wedding cakes that had suddenly been affixed onto the South Boston landscape.

"Battleships," I said.

He nudged me. "Luxury liners."

Without even making eye contact, we mumbled in unison, "Same thing."

Three

❖

Years before, she had the first of many dreams of a line of fire coming from the west; it was no surprise to dream it again now, advancing eastward, unstoppable, destroying everything in its path the whole length of the country, up and down the continent. Somehow she could see this line of fire, even from here at the farthest point east; but maybe here, on the continent's edge, they could jump into the ocean to escape it—this conflagration could not follow them into water, could it? But then what? Then where would they go? And what if the line of fire were propelled by an advancing slick of its own fuel, self-perpetuating? It would pool on water's surface. It would burn there. They would all burn there, in the water. They would not reach another shore in time, even if there were another shore—a harbor island, a cruise ship, a freighter, a barge. Martha's Vineyard. Ireland. Spain. No, they would not reach anything before the fire got there, too. She would be overcome by fire. In a fraction of a second, she knew then: it was over.

"START," I TOLD the people who came to my writing class the first day, my first year teaching at this university, back in the old millennium, "wherever you can, wherever you have something to say, wherever you can just say something. Don't wait until you've found the beginning. Just start writing wherever you are."

The two sad-eyed Eritrean doctors smiled at me, amused and forgiving and yet doggedly unconvinced.

17

"It may feel like it's somewhere in the middle," I persevered. "But it may turn out, in the end, to be the beginning after all."

But the Eritreans never came back to that class. I met them by chance in the hallway a few weeks later. "We are sorry," said Mesfin, the one with the more irregular features, a face crinkled with humility and warmth. "We cannot do it the way you suggest. You know, we spent fourteen years at war, on the front lines. We never studied, we never wrote. Now we need so much time to catch up. There is so much to read for all our courses." He glanced down at a briefcase bulging with textbooks and photocopies and notes.

"Read less of it," I chirped. "Skim. Look at introductions, look at conclusions, decide what you really need before you bother with the middles." But there I was again, unremittingly American, full of efficiencies and extremities.

Berhe shook his head, his eyes bright and bemused. His face was more finely chiseled than his colleague's, a deeper, richer hue. Both men had lost half their adult lives patching up bodies, sending them back into an interminable civil war. "We need it all. We missed everything, you know. We have no choice now but to start at the beginning and go all the way through."

Then I was the one who smiled sadly.

He tacked on an admission. "It's too much. Every night I fall asleep reading."

"You have to sleep," I said. "You're a mature man. Not one of these kids." I gestured to the frighteningly young medical students—children!—who passed us by.

I teach on the medical campus of a big university and often find myself wandering the hallways of the university hospital, following the painted lines on the floor in search of the cafeteria. I'm a writer in some sort of residence but certainly not the sort of residence that all the other residents who wander these hospital halls reside in. The students in my department of public health are culture-shocked doctors and public officials from countries we call "developing," relief workers and former Peace Corps volunteers and other good-hearted Americans out of synch with the times, long out of school. And we require that these most unlikely of all candidates buckle down and write in a style to which no one is accustomed. Not even me. But I am supposed to help.

"You have to pick a topic you're in love with," I told the Thesis Seminar as I began my second year, after I'd been taught by the students in my first. "Your research will go badly sometimes, your hypothesis may prove to be wrong, the foundation of your argument may wobble, your advisor may throw irrelevant questions at you, and though your fourth draft as it comes out of the printer may seem to you a work of genius, polished and ready to submit, two days later it may very well strike you—or somebody else—as moronic. But you will have to persevere. You will have to live with this paper, this mercurial presence, for at least a year. It will turn out well in the end, but to endure its betrayals and tantrums, you will have to love your topic very much indeed."

THAT SAME YEAR, years ago, while I was still taking in the ways my students saw things, a visitor from the International Monetary Fund lectured to an assembly of the whole department. He put forth a steady gush of white-man babble, like a stream swollen from rain, while the air in the lecture hall crackled with the anger and resistance of the listeners. The man had an exaggerated mid-American nasal twang and spewed out twisted vowels like toxic particles into the foamy effluent of his talk.

He concluded a section of his lecture. "And so clearly, structural adjustment has been a success in Ghana."

A student from Ghana shot up her hand, but he did not call on her.

"And now there's the issue of gender and adjustment," he said. "Who's even thinking about it? you might ask. Well, some of *us* have started to think about it."

A low current of female tittering eddied through the room.

"Some of us," shouted Thandi, from Botswana, who already had a PhD, "have been thinking about it for many years!"

"Shush!" called out the bearded man in the front row, a man wearing a turban and a long grayish robe, a doctor from an Afghanistan still ruled then by Taliban.

Sam, the chairman of our department at the time, stood up. "Please have the courtesy to let Mr. Goodrich speak—" A general murmuring made him pause.

And just then Florence, a large woman from Nigeria, entered the lecture hall late, very late, inexcusably late, how did she dare? The door closed behind her with a groan. The murmuring stopped. It was impossible not to look at her. She smiled, oblivious to the mood in the room. She wore a long, bright gold print dress, split up one side to her ample knee; her head was wrapped festively in bright gold cloth. She glanced around the rows, looking for a seat.

"There will be time for questions when he finishes," Sam continued, taking advantage of the lull Florence's entry created. "So please hold your comments until then!"

Florence strode slowly up the long aisle to the back row, still oblivious, still smiling, her composure unruffled, then crossed over to the other side of the hall. Her languor, her smile, her sweet perfume, too, permeated the whole room like a deep, soulful humming, issuing out over us all, even over the lecturer, though he didn't know it, in a delicate, erotic ripple.

"Any questions?" our speaker asked, distracted, absentminded as he scrolled backwards then forwards then backwards again through the dozens of frames of his PowerPoint show, trying to find where he'd left off.

The woman from Ghana raised her hand and did not wait to be recognized. She said, "Since we got structural adjustment, people have had to pay cash for mosquito bednets. They can't afford it. Children are dying more and more from malaria: that is your structural adjustment success story."

The man from the International Monetary Fund nodded. "Thanks for your contribution. Did I see another hand?"

IT TOOK VERY little time for me to understand that *our* students were not just any old students. And every so often, though not very often, there's been a classroom buzz, a true chemical spark on some very dry intergalactic, interplanetary, international, intergenerational tinderbox of desire. It is not supposed to happen for me, a professor, with students, certainly not *my* students, even the ones here so close to my own middle age. But it happens now and then. I punch it down, like a bowl of rising bread dough, and let it do its gentle fermentation out of sight, covered with the damp dishtowel of my professional reserve. Eventually lust bubbles away, my interest leavened by quiet, steady affection. Still, the classroom air was just a tiny bit charged during the spring of 2001, the last semester when the world still felt whole, my own pulse and wit just a bit quicker, all the students just a little more alert. We were energized somehow when Ibrahim was there.

"Due to the fact that," I said.

"Because!" cried out Katherine from Kenya.

"In the event that," I said.

Three seconds of silence passed, then: "If!" That time it was Nayar from Mongolia.

"At this point in time."

"Now!" sang a chorus.

"You see," I said, "you already possess ways to reduce the wordiness and at the same time express things more clearly, without sacrificing an iota of your concept or its complexity. That's at least one easy step to whittling down your draft to the twenty page limit."

"But Professor," said Ibrahim. "For some of us, wordiness is not the problem. For me, if I am not permitted to use phrases like these"—he gestured with a sweep of his long fingers to the page of taboo verbiage on his desk—"then I will never be able to even reach twenty pages."

The class of mostly over-writers laughed.

"What if I can make my whole argument in just ten?" he asked, his eyes sparkling. "Ten pages with sufficient evidence to support each claim, but no wasted words, no jargon. Won't they tell me that it's not academic enough? That it's not professional enough?"

"We will see when the time comes," I replied. "You may be right. But we will see who *they* are. We will see what the ten pages say, and who you have identified as your *audience*." I have always been very big on audience.

When the class session ended, Ibrahim followed me to my office, frowning. He sat down before I even ask him to. He had a scent I could not smell but which I knew was there. A pheromone. Like a little lasso, rounding me up and pulling me to him.

"I thought I had found the perfect match, the object of my desire," he began. His mouth frowned, but his bright brown eyes shone warm and cheerful from behind the oblong lenses of his glasses. My heart fluttered stupidly.

"But I am no longer in love," he sighed, unwinding a long scarf from his neck and drawing his chair closer to me. Elbow on my desk, he rested his majestic square chin in his hand. "I need your advice desperately."

"Yes Ibrahim, I am here to help you."

"That's good. I thought I was deeply in love, but I'm not." A mischievous half-smile twisted his mouth both up and down.

"Ibrahim, your wife and the children are in the Emirates?"

"Professor Erika, yes. That is where they are. Abu Dhabi. They will be here during the holiday break, *insh'Allah*." His whole face lit up.

"But you have fallen out of love?"

Again he frowned. "Yes, Professor, I have fallen out of love with my topic."

"Aha, with your topic."

"My topic," he repeated. "The refugee issue is no longer working for me. It is no longer lighting my fire."

"Yes, the refugee topic." I let a long pause occur. It was me, after all, who had given the be-in-love-with-your-topic lecture. "There is still time to find another topic."

"Yes," he said, "time is what I seem to have the most of here."

As I BEGAN to describe the day's exercise, the students all looked at me, and then away from me, with that conflicted the-teacher-must-be-crazy look, a look I knew very well. It appeared on faces whenever I introduced freewriting.

"You could not do this in Japanese," said Akiko.

"Maybe not," I conceded. "But can you explain why?"

She laughed. "All our days in school, we are told never to say whatever first comes into our heads."

"Never to not think," echoed Zhang.

"Purposelessness," said Ibrahim, "is a luxury. It is not taught in all places."

"But there *is* a purpose!" I countered. "You will see. I agree, the whole idea of it is very American. So write in English if that makes it easier. But if it's more natural for anyone to write in your first language, that's fine, too."

"Even if *you* don't know the language?" asked Zhang.

"I don't read your freewriting pieces. They're private. You have the choice to talk about what you've written when we discuss the exercise, but no one else sees what you've done. So any language is fine."

"And if we spend ten minutes writing and say nothing?" questioned Ramesh. "What good is it? Isn't it a waste of time?"

"Trust me. It is good. Because otherwise I know you will spend ten minutes not writing at all. It is important that you write sometimes in your normal voice, without feeling like every word must be a golden nugget, without that anguished hunt for the perfect phrase. It is important that you get used to throwing words away, to writing not-your-best and reworking it. So after you 'waste' the first ten minutes, I will ask you to spend another ten minutes saying nothing again. Or maybe you will suddenly find yourself saying something."

"I am a professional man," sighed Ramesh. "I spent years learning, *cultivating* how to think very carefully. This assignment is so . . . so undignified."

"Okay. Then write that. Keep writing that. See if it takes you some place."

"Write *what*?" He still didn't get it.

"Write about what a bad assignment this is."

"So we write anything?" asked Ibrahim, sounding more willing, slightly amused, more in the spirit of the task.

"Anything."

"And you won't read it?" He wriggled his eyebrows.

"Not a word of it."

"This is just so high school," said Alice, an American.

"But now you should have more interesting thoughts in your head than you did in high school." I was undaunted by the class's disapproval. "Get your paper and pen ready, please. You do not have to write fast, but you do have to write without stopping. If I see anyone stopping, anyone whose pen is not moving and who's searching for a word, I will hit you and humiliate you in front of all the others."

They laughed. By now they knew I would do no such thing. But they knew I would do *something*.

"Please start." Earnestly, they all began scratching lines on a page. This is what I liked best, those first seconds when twenty thinking adult people from every corner of the planet started freewriting, the momentary sensation that I have set the whole world free.

Only once was a student completely unable to freewrite, refusing to even fake it: a high-strung doctor from Belarus who we later learned was a serious heroin addict well connected to his country's government. He of course could not let himself go. More often, people couldn't stop: I would say *stop* and they would keep writing. I used to think this was good until a handsome young Bangladeshi pharmacist who couldn't stop came up to me after class in a state of deep existential disarray.

"I found myself writing that my life was empty," he blurted. "Suddenly, as I was writing, I knew that everything I have ever done is worthless. I wrote that. All my life has been worthless, except for having my son, and now his mother won't let me see him. There is nothing else worth living for. She has killed me. I wrote that! I didn't even know I thought that!" Tears welled up in his eyes. I sat with him for an hour after class, moving him slowly on to other, happier thoughts. He was okay. Not too long after, he graduated, he fought for custody, he lost, he got a good job with a big pharmaceutical company in Virginia and moved south instead of going back to Bangladesh.

"Stop," I said. Eventually everyone stopped. "Look over what you've written." A few of them had gone well onto a second page. "How did it go? Did you say anything interesting?"

"I had no trouble keeping it up," said Katherine. "But nothing interesting came out. I wrote about all the things I should be doing, it's like a long, long list."

"I wrote about my topic," boasted Ramesh. "It's practically a full problem statement. I can read it if you want."

"Thanks, but not now," I said. "What else?"

"I wrote about personal things." Zhang blushed. "Angry things."

"I wrote very easily about how hard it is to write," said Ibrahim. "My own eloquence surprises me, now that I read it." He did not wait for me to draw conclusions. "Maybe it is not so hard after all."

"First I wrote about lunch," said Alice. "Then I suddenly moved on to a different topic."

"Dinner?" asked Ramesh. There was a bit of tittering, but Alice looked very serious and it stopped. Respect for Alice, even as she flailed and floundered from week to week, was the class's way of kicking Ramesh's superior little ass.

"No. Trafficking of children in Nepal. Suddenly I remembered something I read." She flushed, talked faster. "Suddenly I knew that *this* would be my topic."

THE SHEIKH HAD been good to him, but Ibrahim's wife and kids were stuck in Abu Dhabi, while Ibrahim was stuck here in the States with the sheikh's kid. Tapped to be his personal pediatrician, Ibrahim moved the boy, as if it would do any good, from hospital to rehab, rehab to hospital, or tended to him in the big apartment next to his own when something came up that the household of nurses couldn't handle, seeing him through seizures, bed sores, feeding tube mishaps. He was paid handsomely to take charge of this static shell of a child, while his own four ferociously bright and lively and ever-growing, ever-changing kids did without him. This was the aching irony of his life. (The first irony, that is.) His own true day-to-day existence proceeded without him back in Abu Dhabi, a home which he had hoped would be only a stopover before they could return safely to Khartoum. A stopover that had so far lasted twelve years. All the children were born in Abu Dhabi. Now he was exiled even from the stopover, at the bidding of the sheikh, to pretend a barely flickering child could be rekindled, made whole in the great hospitals of the United States. Bored to death, so much lonely time on his hands—no wonder he decided to go to school.

"Think of your first draft," I told the class, "as a loose sack spread out on a table. A burlap sack, like one you might carry potatoes in. You write a rough section of the paper, it's a nice big potato you throw into the sack. You write another piece, and it goes into the sack. Little by little, you have a sizable collection of potatoes in the sack, which still sprawls out on the table, bulging and bumping unevenly with its many potatoes. Now it's time to take them to market. You take the sack from the table and shake all the potatoes together in the bottom."

I lifted up the imaginary sack by the sides of its slack open top and I demonstrated, shaking it.

"That's the first revision. The sack still isn't full, so you find the potatoes that really fit best in the remaining space—you don't have to look for a thousand more potatoes, just the ones that fit now—and maybe this is the additional bit of research you have to do to bolster your argument, the examples from comparable situations"—I reached out and picked up an imagined tuber from my right side and dropped it into the imaginary bag—"the relevant data that just got published"—I reached to my left—"the answer, finally, to the question you sent an expert months ago"—I reached forward, picked up the imagined round shape, turned it over with a satisfied grin, and placed it gently near the top—"those potatoes fill the bag. And then you pull on the drawstring at the top, *you tighten* it"—and this action, too, I demonstrated with a big to-do of hunched shoulders and strenuous effort of my arms—"and the bag takes its final shape, everything fitting together as tightly and smoothly as possible." I made the motions of tying the loops of a drawstring. "That nice firm sack of potatoes that you bring to the market: that's your final paper.

"But what you have here now, so far," I said, tapping on Katherine's pages, "that's way before you pull the drawstring. These are excellent potatoes, but they have so much useless space around them, they have not yet found their precise place in the denser, tightened heft of the whole sack."

"But Professor," ventured Ibrahim. He sighed. "So many of us prefer rice."

"*Ugali*," said Katherine.

"Bread," said Alice, grimacing.

"Rice," said Nayar.

"Bulghur," said Nada.

"*Foufou*," added Mamadou.

"Rice," whispered Zhang.

"*Nshima*," said Lindiwe. "That's mealy meal."

"Couscous," declared Aisha.

"Rice," said Ramesh. "Basmati rice."

"Rice," said Akiko, starting to giggle out of control. She hid her face in her hands.

Ibrahim smiled warmly at Akiko, then looked straight at me, his face becoming serious. "You cannot tighten rice in a burlap sack," he said.

"THINK OF YOUR argument," I told the class another time, "as a bridge between two riverbanks: you are on one side of a deep, rushing river, and your audience is on the other. You must get your ideas *across* to them. Sometimes, with some topics, to build the bridge you have strong evidence, many solid building blocks, even a surfeit of relevant source material—you may have to pick and choose, to leave some out!—and you can build a firm, wide expanse from one side to the other, each piece of the argument fitting beautifully with the one next to it. (If it's a very wide and solid span, you may wonder: why am I doing this in the first place? Surely this bridge has already been built somewhere upstream? Be sure to check that out.) With other topics, where not much research has been done, where you may have to make judgments or interpretations based on less than complete or obviously relevant data—you can't build that big solid bridge. Maybe not even a rickety rope footbridge. So you might use stepping-stones, but you need enough stones to be able to hop across the river without falling. The stones are the pieces of your argument that are not so clearly connected. Your hops from one to the other are the logic you use to show how they *do* connect."

My students stared at me, wordless. Were they deep in thought or just confused?

"And of course," I lunged forward, "sometimes the other side of the river is very close, and other times it is very far, and you will have to know your audience quite well to figure out which is which and what sorts of building materials you will need to reach it. A stepping-stone argument may work only with a closer riverbank, not a farther one."

Ibrahim cleared his throat. "But Professor, what if there is nothing for a bridge, and all you can do is swim across the river?"

"Then you risk schistosomiasis," I said, pleased that I had my own repertoire of vile diseases—previous students' topics.

He bestowed on me a warm, affectionate smile. Perhaps because I pronounced the word correctly.

"Leptospirosis, maybe, too," added Katherine.

"Or drowneding," said Akiko, her eyes widening with alarm.

"Okay, okay," he said. "I will build."

"THINK OF CITATION and attribution of sources," I said to the class, "as many guests sitting with you at your dinner table, having a feast, having a conversation. When your wife's sister's husband who you haven't seen for many years appears, you don't simply ignore him. Of course not. You invite him to sit down with you. You introduce him. Probably you tell the other guests where he's from and why he's there. He doesn't simply enter the conversation before being introduced."

"Ah," said Ibrahim, clutching his forehead. "You don't know my wife's youngest sister's husband, Sayed. They moved to England. Outside London. We don't see him for years, suddenly he's visiting for a month. To start talking, he never waits for an attribution."

The next class, Ibrahim was absent. And then the next. And then I heard his name spoken in the same breath as a terrible diagnosis—of the child he cared for, certainly? I asked: The sheikh's boy? Must that child endure still more? But no, it was a diagnosis of *him*, of Ibrahim, *our* Ibrahim, the word *pancreas* whispered ever more faintly, always with a wince. Then came talk about surgery for a shunt that could do only temporary good. His wife, Safiya, who had flown in from Abu Dhabi, came to pick up his assignments. She stood in my doorway, tall and dignified in a charcoal tailored pantsuit, stylish pointy-toed red European pumps, a filmy red silk scarf draped over her hair and tossed loosely around her neck. Her sharp, intelligent eyes bright with tears, she identified herself.

I got up to shake her hand, and our hands tightened on each other and could not let go. "How is he doing?"

"He wants to work on his paper." She smiled and gently released my hand. "The children will be on vacation soon and he wants to work on his paper before they get here and take up all his time."

I gave her an envelope with some handouts from the class. "It is not so terrible if he lets it wait. The children are more important. Life is more important."

She kept smiling, while a solitary tear glided down one smooth cheek. "You have all been so good to him here."

Now it was me who fought tears. "Ibrahim is special. So in-sightful. So expansive. But of course you already know that. It is hard to think of him as a student. I would rather think of him as a friend. You and him."

She nodded. We hugged. "Come visit us," she said.

"THINK OF YOUR first draft," I told the class, "as a big lump of clay, the raw material which you have gathered and stuck together in its unwieldy, unshaped form. As you sculpt the clay in the next drafts, it begins to take on the larger shape of your argument, still blocky and coarse and lacking precise definition, but the basic outline and dimensions start to emerge. Finally, with more delicate tools, you are sculpting the more nuanced lines and shapes, the smoothly rounded curves, the exact contours and textures of each element of a fully formed work of art. This is your argument, this fine sculp-ture. This is your final draft."

They stared at me. Nobody spoke. Katherine slumped sideways in her chair. Alice sulked. Zhang smiled blankly, while Ramesh frowned haughtily. Akiko's mouth quivered as if she might speak, but she did not.

"You are sculptors," I said, faltering. I tried to make eye con-tact around the room, but one by one the students averted their eyes. "Yes?" I asked. "You are capable of sculpture?"

Stony silence was their reply.

"You have developed some of those more precise sculpting tools, haven't you?"

They refused to humor me. Finally Akiko said, very softly, "We are waiting for Ibrahim. He is the sculptor."

I let them go early that day. None of us could wait for the semester to end, for the course which we had so enjoyed to finish.

Four

❖

*It was not the sight of bodies tumbling from the towers that stayed
with her so hauntingly, the still-living figures flinging themselves from
unthinkable heights, terrible as they were. What wrenched her off her
hinges was the shot she saw only once: the crowds of people standing
inside at the slits of windows, floor after floor up and down the upper
reaches of the flaming tower. People who could not escape by the stairs,
but who stood at those long, narrow windows, waiting, waiting for
rescue just seconds before the tower fell. That was the sight she could
not drive out of her mind.*

So LOTS OF people have that name, it's not a special name, it's
everywhere. Already I knew people on campus who were Edwards.
Missy Edwards, the reference librarian. Eleanor Hinkleson Edwards,
who taught health economics. Never once did I wonder, is she related to Mr. Edwards. Never once in all those years did I remember
Mr. Edwards.

Toby was still new, a nice young guy, round in the face.
Uncooked. Nothing special, I thought then, and his rapid advance-
ment surprised me later. We talked a little at a going-away party.
There were always going-away parties those days, mostly for women
in the harem who eventually tried to stand up and smacked their
heads hard on the glass ceiling. Each one had been sure she would

move up from program associate to lecturer or program director, into a title with more money and prestige. Each one did her best, then waited a little too long while nothing happened. Now another young woman was leaving when I found myself standing with Toby beside the crackers and cheese. The usual under-ripe Brie and bright orange cheddar, the Triscuits and soda wafers. He was pleasant, undistinguished, with not much to say. I asked him how his first weeks were going. "Good," he said. "There's a learning curve, but I'm incentivized." Probably I winced, hearing those trendy phrases, those semantic ID cards of the upwardly eager. He didn't notice. "It's all a matter of making good on the deliverables." He loaded up a Triscuit with slices of cheddar, packed it all into his round face, and chewed, smiling.

A few days later when he sent a message to the department mailing list and the name Toby Edwards stared out from my in-box, it registered for me finally that his last name was Edwards, and at the exact same second my stomach did a summersault. I broke into a sweat. My heartbeat switched to the palpitation channel. *The son.* Somewhere at the molecular level I already knew; in my muscle and bone and blood the connections had already been made beside the cheese and crackers, the recognition accomplished. I say this in the passive voice, which I am always haranguing against, because I did not do these things in the usual sense of my own agency and will. My gut was way ahead of my brain. As is so often the case. The knowledge was already there, its stranglehold on my gut tightening from surprise and absolute certainty and dismay as soon as I saw the name. *The son.*

THE FACTS I glean from old newspaper and book accounts bear out the deeper knowledge in my gut: Indeed Toby has two older sisters. He is in fact exactly the age he would be if he were who I'm sure he is. He grew up in the New Jersey town *the son* grew up in. In casual talk with him and always with others around, I gradually, reluctantly prove to myself that I am right.

He seems like a nice enough guy. But of course so did his dad. Does the apple fall far from the tree? Is he, perhaps, a chip off the old block?

He would have been ten. The prosecution demanded that he be called as a witness at the trial, but once on the stand he said nothing; his sisters refused to speak, too. A court order could force them to be present, but nobody could make them talk. The poor children! They pull at my heartstrings, even now. But what did confused, terrified little Toby *not* say in court? What did he know or not know? What did he see his own father do? I am crazy with wondering. Did Toby only know the harmless unbaked nebbish I once knew, or did he know the monster, too? Could he possibly have stayed in touch with the man?

No. I am certain that Toby has had no contact with his father since the arrest sixteen years ago. The mother separated from Mr. Edwards as fast as she could, and the divorce was final within weeks of the trial. To go on with their own lives, the children would have had to make the cleanest possible break. I think.

"Hi there, Erika," he greets me in the hallway early in the morning when often we are both in the department before any of the others. Normally slump-shouldered like his dad was, he'll stand up straighter for this greeting, a big cheerful smiley-face grin on his face, another on his favorite coffee mug.

"Hi there, Toby," I reply. For a few weeks, those words are the sum total of our daily conversation. But later on, his "Hi there!" is sometimes lackluster, his grin just a faint quiver of the lips, his shoulders always in a slump.

"Did the baby keep you guys up last night?" I ask.

"Naah. Not really," he says, distracted, his face a blank. When he looks like that, I don't know if he is pensive or sad or just worn out. I feel for him, for the heavy heart that must sometimes make itself felt when he least expects it.

I will never tell Toby I know his darkest secret, the horrors in his extraordinary childhood that he must have struggled all these years to put behind him, to make himself into this bland white-bread adult. (Does he have any idea how much he resembles his father? Is there anyone else on earth right now besides me who would know that? Only the grandparents from whom he has likely been estranged for many years, who have not seen him grow into what he now is.) No matter how sympathetic I might be, if he knew that I knew, it would mean that someone right here at work, all the time and at any time, could blow his cover. My sheer existence would throw his ugly secret into his face every time we passed in hallways, at going-away parties, at waits for the photocopy machine or cof-feepot, at staff meetings. Even at Christmas celebrations, with the wife and baby in tow, there I would be, shaming him, haunting him. He would wonder if I were wondering if he were a murderer, too. And maybe he would be right. He would watch for signs that I was watching for signs. And maybe he would detect them. No, I can't tell Toby, I can't tell anyone. I am locked into a secret that I never chose and absolutely do not want. The coincidence of our crossed paths has struck me from out of the blue like an incurable disease, and I am marooned in it all by myself.

I feel pity for him, first. Then I feel protective—maternal, even. I want to shelter him from *me*, from what I know but wish I didn't. I don't want to force back on him the nightmare past that he has fought so hard to dispel in this hard-won predictable present. He seems to have had a shot at a normal life, however boring or bland, and never would I knowingly disturb a hapless stranger's inner peace. (Or so I *think*.)

So every time we pass in the hallways or hover over someone finishing up at the photocopy machine, waiting our turns, Toby is unaware that I am haunting him. And he is unaware that he and his father are haunting me. As the weeks go on, I lay eyes on Toby across a conference table and I see a bloody ax instead of his yellow legal pad, I smell flesh burning in a lab incinerator. I meet Toby at the recycling bin and notice the torn sleeve of a blood-stained jacket poking out from the bundles of discarded paper. We listen together to the last shudders of a brewing coffeepot, and I hear muffled screams, watch a fat, pale hand struggling to cover a lipstick-red mouth. Waiting beside Toby at the elevator, I see disembodied knees and arms and a female torso occupying the spaces where weavings and masks and paintings usually hang on our vestibule walls.

My compassion has spared Toby from a haunted life, from a meltdown at his new job. But look at what's happening to *me*, here in the placid summer of 2001.

Then he comes to my doorway to announce that a plane crashed into Tower 2, and again the violence streams at me from everywhere: local and global, personal and political, it's all unleashed. My ability to differentiate falters.

Five

She looks up into the sky and sees a five-pronged asterisk-like figure that reminds her of the shape of jacks, a child's game she played long ago with a little red ball (faded to brown, finally, and cracked) and a dozen small, spiky metal pieces. But this image in the sky is not a game, not a toy, no, nothing like a toy; it must be a very large object, now growing even bigger and more ominous. The sky itself grows darker and threatening. She freezes in terror. Then she sees another one, and still another, and then many others appear, these things in this shape that move closer and grow larger, filling the sky. And by then, when it is too late, she knows that Boston is under attack, maybe everywhere is under attack, certainly she is under attack, and nobody is protecting them. Nothing will be done to stop the attack and any minute now the world will be devastated, she will be gone. Even sobbing herself awake, she knows it is all coming to an end.

IT'S NOTHING-TO-LOSE TIME all the time now. I am a real pro when it comes to last-gasp futile effort. I take it upon myself to say to the dean, "So many of us told you we don't want Nussbaum for department chair. He's a bully. We'd prefer a search and to take our chances on an unknown. You didn't listen to what we said. And now we're quite certain you'll appoint him anyway. So those meetings come off as a charade. Morale stinks worse now than ever. I think you should meet with us all as a group so we can hear each other, too, for once, before you announce it. Deal with the bad morale before it's a fait accompli."

The dean turns bright angry red and splutters, "This is hardly the time. What do you mean I didn't listen? The nerve of you. I had more than twenty meetings, one by one. And it was not, as you seem to think, unanimous. You all had your chance. You of all people should understand it's far too late now. I'm really surprised at you. Disappointed, that you, *you*, would behave so badly."

I tell no one but Ivan. "Ouch," he says, wincing. "That's a reprimand if ever there was one. Why'd you do that to yourself? You knew he'd already decided long before."

But the announcement is postponed, first one week, then two. The dean calls a meeting with the whole department. Everyone clears their calendars and comes. We have our say again, this time all of us together. Even the ones who sort of *like* Nussbaum think appointing him chair is a bad idea. He's a micromanager, he's a control freak, he has terrible social skills: the evidence mounts. The dean seems to be listening, emitting well-timed grunts, uh-huhs, I-sees.

Ivan gives me a little hug when no one is looking. "You never know," he says.

The next day the dean announces he has appointed Nussbaum the new chair.

AFTER HIS CORONATION, Nussbaum rarely comes to see me, but when he does he makes sure I am sitting and he is standing, so as to appear taller than me, which he is not. He runs his hand back from his forehead through his thick blond hair, then tugs at his bushy goatee.

"Hey, Erika, we need your help on a project. Toby has a proposal due to go out to the Institutes of Health on Thursday and he could use a hand with the writing."

It is already Wednesday. I have preparations for my two courses on Thursday and a dozen drafts to comment on between now and then. Besides, I am not a writer for the department, I am a professor, a writing *teacher*. "I don't think so. I have two classes tomorrow and papers to read, too."

"Hey, just this once. Toby has been up to his ears in reports for the Botswana portfolio and he could use a hand with this one proposal."

"I don't know anything about this project." Of course I don't know anything about *any* project.

"All you have to do is help with the *writing*. You don't have to know the project."

This guy really thinks the two are separate. "So Toby will do the knowing and I will do the writing."

"Don't be sarcastic, please. I'm sorry you don't like Toby. But all you have to do is help with the *writing* part."

"I don't *don't* like Toby. This has nothing to do with liking Toby or not liking Toby. Why wouldn't I like Toby?" I ask. But suddenly I wonder, why *would* I? Why on earth would I actually *like* Toby? Right then, in the briefest fraction of a second, something in my alchemy shifts; all the ingredients of my protectiveness and empathy get ready to reconfigure into dislike. On your mark, says a little voice in my head. Get set. "It's just that I have a full-time job already."

"So does everybody. Everybody helps out. I'm simply asking you to pull your weight."

Since he became chairman, it is equal opportunity overwork here. If everyone is stretched to the limit, if every employee is pitted against other employees (the more the better), we are all easier to govern and exploit and incentivize and no one will notice how crass and banal he is, how short he is. He has learned this no doubt from higher levels of so-called leadership. It's a national trend.

I go to Toby's office. He grins. "Usually I'm on top of these proposals, but this one got ahead of me somehow." I know that is rubbish. Kate from the harem covered for two others but of course now she has resigned; the party was last week.

While he pulls a chair in from the hallway for me, I look at a photograph on his bookshelf: in it are three undistinguished, pudgy adolescents—two girls and a boy—and a worn-out, washed-out woman of indeterminate age, lumpy around the middle, everything about her from waistband to soul stretched beyond any normal day-to-day wear, its elastic resilience obliterated.

"Is this you?" I point to the boy.

"Yup. And my sisters."

"And your mom?"

"Yeah, that's my mom."

"You look like her," I say. I do *not* say, But you look more like your dad. However, I do say, "So what about your dad?"

Toby doesn't miss a beat. "He died when I was ten."

I *do* miss a beat. One or two. When he was ten. Yes, that was when Mr. Edwards went to prison. "That's too bad."

Toby gives a sickly smirk. "You wanna read what I've got so far?"

I read what he's got. "Not bad for starters. But the needs assessment and justification seem thin to me. I could easily help flesh that section out. Tell me why it's important to observe the exact decrease in per capita family resources in these households after they take in the AIDS orphans if we already know that the *same* resources are divided among *more* household members—"

"*Change* of resources." Suddenly he's uppity. Truly unpleasant. "Not *decrease*. Don't involve yourself in that. Stick to just the *writing*, please," he commands.

The little voice of dislike, the voice inside my head of get ready and get set, now yells the final signal to me, Go! And all at once a gooey stream of antipathy oozes in where every particle of my clean, solid empathy had just been. So what if his father was an ax murderer; Toby's a jerk, perfecting his arrogance at Nussbaum's knee.

"You mean just fitting the words into sentences? The grammar? Is that what you mean? The mechanics? Don't trouble myself with the thinking or logic or—"

Nussbaum sticks his sneering face in the door. "I couldn't help but overhear. This proposal is basically an amendment to a grant we already have; the justification has already been accepted. Long ago. The content is *not* your problem, Erika. Toby is absolutely right. Just help with the *writing*, please. Getting it out the door."

So I am the repairman. The technician fixing up Toby's mal-functioning paragraphs. And I am the chambermaid dealing with the unmade beds of his sentences and the sloppy words he has flung on paper like he might fling his shirt and underwear and wet towels to the floor.

So I read, I edit, I tinker, I tighten. I scribble clarifications and substitutions in the margins. I insert punctuation in page after page where there is no punctuation at all, and I remove jarringly useless commas in a section where they suddenly accumulate, as if all the previously missing ones had been stashed there. In my deepest gut I know that a man who throws commas between a subject and a verb cannot be trusted. Timidly I say, "I don't seem to have the section on the intervention you propose."

He flashes a superior smirk. "There is no intervention."

"You mean the families just get poorer and with all the money you're asking for, there's no intervention? No *help*?"

"We don't *know* they'll get poorer. They may become more resourceful. Or some household members might leave and there'll be more to go around."

"*Leave*? Household members might *leave*? You mean *die*, don't you?"

"We don't know yet. That's what the study's for." He speaks slowly, as if explaining to a child or a simpleton. "When we find out for sure, if that's what we find, then there will be a basis for an intervention. That's already planned for year four."

"This got by the institutional review board?"

"Of course."

I keep my mouth shut. Four years of hunger, no doubt illness and resentment, too, before the study's "subjects" (who are actually its objects, in one of science's interesting semantic flip-flops) get a dime from their well-fed researchers. This is science? This is science. So be it. I try to read only the *words* now, divorced from their significance. I squeeze verbs into pileups of noun phrases. I cross out excessive adjectives and discard redundancies. By late Thursday afternoon, when I come back after my classes, Toby has sneaked many of them back in.

The deadline looms over us like a ceiling lamp swinging from very frayed wires: I have no time for him to catch on—there's no time here for riverbanks or bridges or sacks of potatoes. No time to stress the importance of active verbs or the life-and-death differences between commas and colons. But Toby clings to his sloppy ways every chance he gets. Even when I try to clarify the antecedents of pronouns, he resists. He seems to have a strong attachment to subject-verb disagreements, too. We are stuck in his office Thursday night until half past eleven. I invent an entire set of goals and objectives that I see at the last minute are required in the guidelines but have never been done. As I spew them out and type them up, trying not to involve myself in any *content*, Toby tiptoes into the hallway to eat a sandwich he thinks I haven't seen. I hear him phoning home, barking in choppy phrases. Because he has to get back to the wife and kid, I make the required eight copies and rush them to the post office branch at South Station that stays open until midnight. A guard in the doorway angrily shakes his head "no" at me, gesturing that they are ready to lock up. I run past him as if I haven't seen. For this odious proposal, I am committing a federal offense. With about one second to spare, a merciful clerk stamps today's postmark.

Nussbaum copies me on his email to Toby on Friday morning: "Dear Toby: The proposal looks great. Good work, Toby! Thanks, Toby, for going the extra mile to get it out the door on time."

I can't help myself; I fire off a reply. "Did I miss your thank-you note to *me*?"

In seconds he snaps right back. "That is so unprofessional of you, so *childish*," he writes. "You know very well that Toby is still new and needs encouragement. I'm shocked by your bad behavior."

IT IS LOW tide when we sit out on the seawall steps. Ivan has brought the wine this time, a good Bordeaux. The planes are back in the air, not as many as before; still, every few minutes, one of them drones overhead in its slow-motion descent toward Logan Airport. We can see the colors, distinguish the airline. The globe with its zippy stripes of latitude and longitude on Continental's blue tail. The red body and white cross of SwissAir. The green of Aer Lingus. The sun, meanwhile, is a bright orange ball, preparing to sink behind a stout blockish high-rise at Marina Bay, which sits closer to us and a bit farther west than the downtown skyline, glinting silver.

"It's so beautiful," says Ivan, pouring the wine, "you'd think it was peacetime."

We sip, we watch, we hear.

Ivan suddenly stands up, goes to the bottom of the steps and walks out onto the rocks and shells that would be deep under water at high tide. He tests out his footing in leather shoes. He is dressed in light blue shirtsleeves and olive corduroys. He loosens his tie. He begins to dance by himself on the wet stones, slick with seaweed, his large, pushing-sixty body surprisingly graceful and lithe as he skips sideways, bends low to one side and then the other, dipping one shoulder, raising it, dipping and raising the other, his neck and head in constant, slow fluid movements. Then his feet begin to criss-cross and stomp a complicated, measured but melody-free maneuver along the stones.

"Is that a Zorba dance?" I ask.

"No. An Uzbek dance, a peasant dance, an Uzbek folk dance." He snaps the fingers of his left hand, holding his half-empty wine glass high in the air with his right hand, humming, twirling slowly, humming faster, twirling faster, then twirling slowly again until he stops. But not for long. He crouches down stiffly, arms folded in front of his chest, and manages to kick out one leg, then the other, again and again, the wine sloshing out of his glass and the sky streaking a last hurrah of orange and purple behind him. A very loud US Airways Boeing 737 passes overhead.

Then he rises from his crouch, twirls halfway in one direction, halfway in the other. "Of course I'm faking it," he shouts. Then he laughs. He swallows the last drop of wine. He stomps his foot, jerks his head from side to side in rhythm with his stomping. He does some fast-footed lunges. "How would I know an Uzbek folk dance?"

"It's very convincing," I say. "You're a man of many talents."

A heron takes flight, rising up from the tall grasses near the small beach down the road, flapping its huge blue wings. Arms stretched all the way out in a line to each side, Ivan slows down again, dances over to me, and hands me the wine glass so he can snap the fingers of both hands, which very gradually speed up as he does his fancy sideways steps back out along the edge of sea grass. The grasses are just beginning to tinge, already fading to autumn yellows. A Delta flight with its red-bordered blue tail begins its final descent. Ivan flaps his long wings. He flutters out of his Uzbek dance into a heron dance, running, swooping down toward the grass, then up again, his shoulders undulating as he runs, light as air. I almost expect to see him rise into the sky. Suddenly he stops and stands on one foot, stretching his neck upward. He holds the pose, a potbellied human heron silhouette. A sculpture. I hold my own breath. Behind him now the orange disk is gone, the Boston skyline reflects a few last golden sparkles, and then gradually turns smoky blue. Ivan stands on two feet now, loosens his shoulders and flutters his bent wings, arms close to his sides now. The wings flap and ruffle more quickly, still at his sides, impatient. Then he slowly stretches out his arms again, sways and curls them up and down, curling his wrists, undulating to the left, then to the right, then upward. The two hands meet over his head. They stay there. Suddenly they explode in a clap. A single clap. He stops perfectly still for almost a full minute, leaning ever so slightly to the left. His tie flaps in a light sea breeze. Air Canada with its maple leaf hums above us. Gulls squawk from the shore. Finally, above his head, he begins to snap his fingers slowly, then faster, his feet begin to move, his phony Uzbek dance begins again, heading back toward me along the slick stones, sure-footed.

"A NEW DISASTERS course," says Sam, the old chairman. "That's what we can do!" Now he gets so fired up at the department's faculty meeting, he actually closes his laptop and looks around the conference table as if noticing us for the very first time. I hold my breath: he had grown tired, he had stepped down after more than a decade at the helm, and after that he wrote emails during meetings, distant and distracted and silent. But now, suddenly, right before our eyes, he is sparked by a sudden brainstorm. Excited, even, after these last years of personal doldrums and decline: he leans forward, energetic beads of sweat erupting on his face.

"We can offer it to firefighters, cops, EMS workers everywhere. Apply what we already know from the international scene. A three-week summer course. Or maybe two weeks. Or four weeks. We'll see. Market it like crazy. What an opportunity! A goldmine! We've already got the people to teach it. Every frontline emergency crew in the country should take this course." The stripes are nearly leaping from his tie. He is inspired by terrorism, downright giddy, rejuvenated by the boundless opportunities the attacks have opened up.

"Isn't there already a federal agency for that?" asks Fiona, who always has at least one foot on the ground. "Like FEMA, for instance?" Her bangs hanging partway in her eyes, she grins in her girlish way, which confuses people.

"Well FEMA *is* pretty limited," Nussbaum interjects, plucking at his beard. He rarely comes to the defense of Sam, whom he despises. So he must see something big in this for himself. Or his disdain for Fiona outdoes his hatred for Sam. Or both. Yes, there may be double rewards here for Nussbaum; he's hit the jackpot. "Besides, we've got the academic cachet."

"The experience. The international know-how," says Sam.

"The international *market*," says Nussbaum.

"Won't visas be harder to get?" asks Fiona. "For foreign students, I mean. Don't you think a crackdown is on its way any day now?"

"It's all in the marketing," says Nussbaum, as if neither Fiona nor her words exist.

"How about the teaching?" I ask. "Isn't it all in the teaching?"

"A brand," says Toby. "*Our* brand." What a cheerleader he has become. "Nobody else comes close when it comes to short courses."

How on earth would he know? I wonder. He has never worked in any of our courses; certainly he has never taken any. And what is he doing at a faculty meeting anyway?

"I think Sam is onto something here," says Abby, always the fond lapdog, looking up from her elaborate crosshatched doodling in the margin of the agenda. Next to her, Ben is reading the *New England Journal of Medicine*. Behind him, Sally has somehow managed to avoid the conference table altogether and records grades from a pile of student assignments stacked on the chair beside her. Horst busies himself with the keyboard of a handheld device. Bob appears to be sleeping with his eyes open. Meanwhile, the runaway train of bad ideas chugs along faster and faster toward the precipice.

"We could have it up and running by summer," says Sam. "The market is endless. Bet we could fill it two or three times a year. Keep the price down. The international people will come, too. Mark my words. The beauty of it is, the threat is damn near universal."

"Oh yes, that's really beautiful," I say, sotto voce. Fiona starts to giggle and hides her face in her hands. Ivan pushes an elbow into my shoulder.

I elbow him back. "Say something," I whisper. "*Stop* them. *You* they'll listen to. A *man* needs to step in here."

He frowns.

I write the word CO *WARD* large on my agenda page and push it over to him. He pushes the same word back to me, back *at* me. Then he scrawls, *Feminist??? You???*

"Somebody better run it by the dean before we commit any substantial faculty time," says Nussbaum. "The school admin may already be planning something on the public health response."

"Good idea," says Sam.

"Good idea," echoes Toby.

"So who'll follow up?" asks Fiona, relentless with her pesky out-loud drubbings of reality.

Now silence hangs like a dark, noxious cloud over the table.

"I'd be on a committee," offers Toby, finally.

"Thanks, Toby. And obviously Sam," says Nussbaum.

Sam acquiesces with a reddening face and silent smirk.

"Okay, you can count me in, too," says Abby.

Ivan whispers to me, "Whew, at least nobody'll ever follow up."

"This little baby ain't goin' nowhere," I whisper back.

SAM LUMBERS FAST down the long hallway like a man possessed, tie aslant, shirt buttons straining, jacket dribbled with something from lunch, trousers too tight around the belly and thighs. From inside my office I can hear his panting and the thudding impact of his large racing feet. These days, especially after the idea of the disasters course so quickly bit the dust, he seems to always hurtle past in a heavy blur. He does not wear clown's shoes or a clown suit or a big painted smile or a bulbous red nose, and he is not a clown, he is a serious and brilliant man with a distinguished career, now mostly behind him. But as soon as I think of a clown, it is hard not to think of a clown, hard not to think of *him* as a clown. First it was anthrax. Then it was SARS. Then it was smallpox. Then it was the Ebola virus. Then it was anthrax again. Then it was the flu strain from the pandemic of 1918 that still hides out in somebody's lab. Now it's smallpox again. The terrorists will try to get us all with *an infectious disease*. If he can figure out which one it will be, he can not only get *on* the defensive bandwagon, he can *drive* it. He won't need the fickle department or the school behind him, either. Now he's certain it's smallpox. It's perfect. There's not much he can do about dirty bombs, attacks on LPN gas facilities or nuclear plants, hijackings, or seaport infiltrations. But smallpox is right up his alley. He has begun testifying to congressional committees, international conferences, UN agencies, assemblies of survivalist crackpots in Idaho, anyone who'll listen: bioterrorism is the next big thing, the weapon of choice. And smallpox makes so much sense: so easy to spread far and so fast; a few suicide transmitters on planes and trains could set the epidemic in motion all over the world before anyone even caught on.

No one has died anywhere on earth from smallpox for years. Everyone really *is* dying from malaria, TB, AIDS.

The terrorists have won.

"Sam will co-teach the advanced seminar with you next semester," Nussbaum tells me, suddenly appearing beside my desk, trying to look tall with his blond hair slicked upward. "I want somebody who can work more with students on the substance, the *content* of their papers in that class."

"Fiona has been teaching with me just fine for the last two years. She's got plenty of substance. Why fix what's not broken?"

He tries to smile, but a sneer emerges. "Fiona, if you must know, feels like second fiddle in the course. She's restless."

This doesn't make sense to me. "How is that possible without my knowing?"

"Well, *duh*, would she tell *you*, if you're part of the problem?"

"What problem?"

He laughs. "Your not even knowing there's a problem, *that's* a problem. Anyway, I have other things in mind for Fiona next semester. And you could use some gender balance in that course."

I'm nearly speechless. "*My* course is where we suddenly need gender balance?"

Now he frowns. "I'm really surprised you aren't jumping with joy at the chance to have Sam's experience and expertise in the class. Surprised and disappointed."

I have recently become an unquenchable font of disappointment. How did that happen? "You know that Sam is a raving lunatic these days. All he can talk about or think about is smallpox."

"So make smallpox one of the topics in the course."

"But the students pick the topics." I get up from my desk and, knowing he can't see my feet, stand on tiptoe. "You know very well the course revolves entirely around their research and what they're writing."

He scowls, senses I am taller than he is, and backs away. "I'm sure you and Sam will figure it out." Cutting off any further protest, he scoots out the door.

Poor Nussbaum. He doesn't know what to do about me. I am getting old. I don't want anything I can't have. I am not in the vortex of the field and have nothing *he* wants. My only ambition is to teach, which is what I already do. Nussbaum can't get a handle on that: if I have nothing for him, what good am I? And if I have no ambition, how will he manipulate me? But he has finally figured it out. He can screw up my teaching.

For a while I avoid Fiona. We pass in the hall and both avert our eyes. But she is my friend. Or at least she has been my friend up until now. Finally I go to her office and sit down. She closes her door and sits facing me. Her bangs are freshly trimmed, her forehead smooth.

I blurt it out. "Is it true you feel like second fiddle and don't want to teach the seminar with me anymore?"

Now the forehead ripples as she stares at me with unfaked bewilderment. "Who says I don't want to teach the course? I love our course. You *know* I love our course."

"Nussbaum told me that you're restless, you want out, that I'm too dense to see there's a problem, and he has other plans for you next semester."

"*What?*" She throws her head back and swivels around in her chair a full three hundred and sixty degrees. She clutches her temples like a major migraine has suddenly hit. "Doesn't he know we *talk* to each other? How could he lie like that? He told *me* that you wanted to try it with Sam next time. *I* was hurt!"

"Sam is a stark raving lunatic. Who would want him in their classroom? Not me. But Nussbaum is forcing me to teach with Sam."

"I'd give anything to stay in the course," says Fiona.

"He doesn't understand friendship, does he?" I ponder. "He has no clue that there are relationships between people that involve trust and candor. He thinks we're all motivated by the same petty rivalries and greed that motivate *him*. He figures that you and I will walk around pissed at each other forever, because we both believed his lies."

Fiona frowns. "He wants me to dig up my old management course and help Toby teach it."

"Toby's going to *teach*?" I am shocked.

"And I'm supposed to *teach* him how to *teach*. How to teach *my* course. Which I made from scratch and worked my butt off for, all these years."

She flashes a big, resigned smile at me and gives an exaggerated shrug, her palms up at her shoulders. "Hey. What're we gonna do?"

THIS TIME IVAN does not go home after we finish the bottle of wine out on the crumbling seawall steps, long past sunset. We head inside the darkened house, our hands searching for one another. In the throes of our surprisingly intense middle-aged lust, I grope in the drawer of my night table and pull out a condom.

"No," Ivan says.

"We have to," I insist. "You tell me about this woman and that woman from before. You travel a lot. I travel some. Okay, fine. We don't begrudge the past, and you have your Anya—not to imply she's up to anything in your absence, but we're not stupid. Things happen. We even *teach* about safe sex. We *teach* that when people have more education they have safer sex. So."

"So?"

"You have all those degrees. Even more than I do."

He sighs loudly. "What do you think, I am infected?"

"And what do you assume, that I'm *not*?" I open the condom wrapper. "I haven't been tested lately. Have you?"

He pushes my hand away. I push away his. "Are we doing this or not?"

"I'm a *doctor*, for God's sake, do you think I would go around spreading diseases?"

"You're a *doctor*. Shame on you. All the more reason."

He sighs, very annoyed. "You insist? Okay, *you* do it."

He lies back as if he is no longer participating, as if somehow *I* can use a condom without him, and rests both his hands on the spongy mound of his belly. But his penis, still eager and independent, stands erect for me. Very carefully I begin unrolling the condom downward, but can't prevent it from snapping against him as I fit it on.

"Ouch! What are you doing?"

"I'm so sorry." I continue with a less sure hand.

"You're castrating me!"

"Sorry."

"Ouch!"

I apologize at least eleven times. Finally it is on correctly, though he has shrunk a bit, and then a bit more, and then quite a bit. Now he resumes his lovemaking with brusque caresses, he gets on top, entering me quickly. After a few graceless thrusts, he exclaims, "You're too small!"

"What? I am *not* too small!" I do not say, How could I be too small when you are not, after all, so big?

He returns to the effort, the fast rhythm, abandoning subtlety or nicety. But then he stops. "It's not so good. You're too small."

"Ivan, I am not too small. If there is one thing I have never been, it's too small. Do you mean the condom is too tight?"

He rolls off and away from me. "Something is too small. I need more room." He yanks off the condom and hurls it on the floor.

"Oh for God's sake," I say, in a very hot fluster. I get astride him and guide him into me, condom-free, while he's still half limp, but then he stiffens and I feel him expanding more. I sit fully on him.

"Am I too small *now*?"

"No," he laughs. He kisses my breasts, he licks the nipples, he buries his face between them. "Now you're just right."

Six

❖

For a few days America stopped shopping, but she took the half-empty subway to Filene's. Spooky. The store was a hyper-air-conditioned ghost town, a movie set before the cast and crew got there, only a few sales women visible behind silent cash registers. She fingered quilts, smoothed them with the flat of her hand. Security blankets! She'd cringe at the memory someday. She liked the quilt with an old-fashioned log cabin patchwork design, its heft, the wrinkly texture of some squares, the velours of others, the stitching and knotting, the blue motif. It was too expensive, but she bought it, this cliché of a quilt. On the subway home, a couple of drug addicts stood leaning against the doors even though there were plenty of empty seats; they were talking, their words slurry. Something about the next stop, but no, not the next stop, the next bomb. Was that really what she heard? Bomb? Shoulders against the door, the woman with stringy bleached hair let herself slide down until she was sitting on the grimy floor. The man prodded her in the thigh with his battered shoe and almost fell over. They both laughed, revealing missing teeth. He too slid down so they were sitting side by side. Hey, misery loves company. He took her hand. They were messed up but he took her hand and held it. Erika burst into tears and clutched the dumb blanket in its bag.

EARLY IN THE summer they all came to my house, the four children, too. Ibrahim wore a loose linen shirt that hid his new, diminished contours. He'd brought cards and played a game with the children, then amused us all with card tricks first and riddles next. Safiya wore a long blue dress, an *abaya* heavy with silvery embroidery and slivers of mirror woven into it; it was cut low in front, but the black headscarf covered her throat and neck. Now and then as she talked—and she talked with great animation, being as she was by now, so quickly, in the way she shared with her husband, a most intense and gracious friend—the scarf would slip a bit, and she would slowly, automatically rewrap it, and in the rewrapping, her flawless skin, the skin that no one but her husband was meant to see, was clearly visible. After lunch we watched their wedding video which they had once told me about and I'd asked to see, excerpts from the ceremonies and dancing that went on for days, hundreds of people in attendance. So much festivity! So much food! The women singing and dancing in one room, the men in another. Oh, the bright colors! The silks and chiffons! The intricate patterns painted on Safiya's hands!

"Papa, look!" squealed Nasra. "Look at you *dance*!"

Little Shahira twirled round and round in circles until she fell sideways on the rug in fits of giggles.

He fast-forwarded through more dancing. "Professor Erika will be very bored if we watch it all," he said as Nasra protested.

"We could be here watching for four days," said Safiya, her eyes glued to a lingering image of Ibrahim back then. "We would clean out her refrigerator and all of her cupboards," she joked, unsmiling. My eyes followed hers, and I saw what she saw: Ibrahim not only younger but healthy, robust and filled out, greeting his wedding guests in constant, happy motion. I felt the shock she must have been feeling, I realized, too, how much of him had drained away, so gradually that we barely noticed as it happened. But now we saw how terribly thin and slow he had become.

As we watched the video, his eyes began to close, then snapped open; closed again, opened again. He needed to recharge, to restore some of the energy he had been dispensing all day.

So Safiya and I took the kids out for a walk and let Ibrahim doze on the leather reclining chair. Safiya teetered along the stone beach on very high heels. The kids had been cooped up in their city apartment for a few weeks and now broke loose: they skipped rocks, collected shells, ran way ahead, then back to us, and then ahead again along the shoreline, jubilant in the wind. Breathless, they slowed down, counting planes coming in for a landing in the flight pattern within our view. Safiya and I sat on the rocks, gazing at the Boston skyline across the bay, as little Shahira plopped down on rippled sand and sifted through her pail of shells. Abu dissected a dead crab, Karim dug a hole in the sand, Nasra leafed through a wildlife book, then played catch with Karim after he abandoned his hole. On the way back to the house, the children ran and shrieked along the route again. Inside, Ibrahim was still asleep; Safiya woke him, gently rubbing his shoulder and murmuring into his ear. Shahira clambered into his lap before he was fully awake.

It was time for tea and dessert. They had brought a beautiful fruit tart. I handed the first plate to Nasra, who approached her slice gingerly, with a fork.

His voice thick and raspy, Ibrahim said, "No, Nasra, use your fingers, touch it, get messy if you have to, to truly enjoy things you must use all four of your senses!"

The children all picked up their slices in their hands and gob-
bled into them, unrestrained.

"But how do you *hear* it?" asked Nasra, teasing her father,
holding her plate to his ear. "I don't *hear* mine!"

"Listen to Karim's," said Safiya, "as the pieces hit the floor."
She dispensed paper napkins to the kids, scooped up chunks of
fallen fruit and pastry. "So sorry, Erika."

"It doesn't matter at all!" I said.

Ibrahim grinned. "Professor Erika doesn't mind." He barely
touched his own dessert.

After they left, I sat in the leather recliner, now imbued with
Ibrahim's scent. Sandalwood and lemon. Cinnamon, too.

IBRAHIM'S SISTER OPENED the door because Safiya was not at home.
She spoke no English, this sister Saleha, who was so large and so
devout, swathed in bright oceans of Sudanese cloths from head to
toe, but she gestured to me to sit down and then disappeared for an
instant. Soon Ibrahim stood in the hallway in his plaid bathrobe,
the cuffs of his pajamas peeking out below. He approached the living room with mincing steps, touching the wall to keep his balance.
He pronounced his greetings to me. He would not sit. It hurt more
to sit, he explained. He wanted to be gracious. No, he did not really want to be gracious, but it was so much a part of his nature,
that grace, that expansiveness, that way of putting other people at
ease, that he simply couldn't *not* be gracious. He asked me little
questions; I gave him little answers. I felt it was wrong to force conversation on him, but he insisted on the niceties. His face receded in
shadowed hollows where the fullness used to be.

"Have you spoken by phone to the children now that they're back in Abu Dhabi?" I asked. The three oldest were now in the big, bustling household of Safiya's mother, aunts, and cousins, ready to go back to school, while baby Karim stayed on here.

"Yes, every day, and just this morning, first Nasra, she was so happy because that morning—you know the many hours' difference between here and there—this morning, there, she had—she had—" His voice stuck, and he stopped talking. He tried again to say his older daughter's name, to tell her story, but produced only rasps. His face struggled against a contortion and I realized he had begun to weep. He stood in his bathrobe, emaciated and in pain, thinking of the children whose chatter over the phone, over oceans and thousands of miles, he lived for now. He stood in his bathrobe thinking of them and wept. There was nothing I could do except let him weep; I could not touch him, could not make words, could not stop him or console him. I turned to his sister, who, closed up in her other language, could not say anything to me and would not say anything to him. She smiled briefly and nodded at me, to acknowledge that we were there, we could do nothing but watch Ibrahim standing in his bathrobe, eyes closed, thinking of his children and silently weeping.

At last he mustered enough strength to bear down on his sobs, to stop, to stop again, to open his eyes. He whispered, "How are things at the department? When do classes begin? What is new at school?"

I was only starting to reply when Safiya burst through the front door. She was electric, a strobe light in a neon lime green chenille sweater, clutching too many grocery bags. Her tight jeans revealed curves; her long black hair streamed out unrestrained and uncovered. She was transformed: very young, very fast, a completely Western woman, more like an American teenager than a Sudanese mother of four. Her face was flushed, her big bright eyes shimmering with excitement.

"I did it!" she cried out to us. "I drove to the Star Market all alone!"

Her elation was a perfume that wafted through the room, a perfume she had used profligately. I couldn't miss it, nor could Ibrahim help but catch the scent.

"You had no trouble finding the store?" he asked.

"Of course not! I've gone with you there a hundred times." She released all of the bags onto the floor.

"And the parking?"

"Easy!" She tossed back her hair. "I don't know what all the fuss is about with parking. It's a supermarket with spaces for cars, not Fenway Park."

"Good," he said softly. "Good," he said again, as if trying to convince himself.

Her back to him, Safiya handed bag after bag to his sister to carry into the kitchen. He turned around slowly, but not before his hollow cheeks began glistening with tears. Abandoning grace, unashamed to be weeping again, and forgetting I was there, he retreated to his bedroom without a word.

SITTING ON THE floor at the end of the hospital hall, the old man slowly peeled the orange, lifting the skin away in one ragged piece. He loosened the sections of fruit so they fanned out from the center, the whole still intact. Then gently he pulled off one section and put it in his own mouth. His eyes lit up with laughter as he put another plump orange morsel between Karim's surprised but eager little lips.

A siren wailed relentlessly down below. Ibrahim's mother gestured to me to stand beside her, then pointed to the street.

"Traffic," I said. "Rush-hour traffic." She did not understand English, but I still felt compelled to speak.

She shook her head impatiently, pointing again.

"Oh, the ambulance," I said. "An emergency. It's an ambulance."

She repeated the word. "Alm-boo-lonce." Siren blaring, red light flashing, the ambulance was stuck. No cars tried to move out of its way, and with the street jammed with traffic in every direction, where would anyone have gone?

Ibrahim's mother looked at me with pleading, panic-stricken eyes.

"It's terrible," I said.

The siren seemed to get louder, more insistent. She gasped.

"It's Boston," I said.

"Boston," she repeated. But her eyes said, So what if it's Boston?

Safiya came toward us, her high-heeled shoes clicking a purposeful staccato on the hall floor. Today she was dressed conservatively in loose trousers and a long-sleeved tunic, a black scarf closely covering her head. Barely slowing down, she took only a very quick look inside as she passed Ibrahim's door. She kneeled to kiss Karim and greet her father-in-law, then stood with us at the window. Ibrahim's mother said something to her in Arabic, anguished.

"Halima is disturbed that the ambulance is stuck?" I asked.

"She is asking, 'Why don't those idiots let it through?'" Safiya gave a weary laugh. "She has not been here long enough to know what goes on."

"Tell her that inside the ambulance it's like a small hospital, that there's probably everything in there for the medic to treat the patient."

Safiya translated. The old woman spoke again, a frown sending deeper and deeper furrows into her broad, weathered cheeks.

"She said, 'What if the ambulance is on the way to pick up the patient? What if he is still home, having a heart attack or bleeding to death?'"

Alas, what if. I felt so inadequate. I wanted to reassure her that we do not let people die so easily, so carelessly in this country. But she knew we did. She knew we could do it to her son. "Tell her that probably on this street, heading in that direction, it is on its way to the emergency room entrance, which is on this block. We can only hope."

Safiya translated. As Ibrahim's mother spoke, I could make out the words: *Insh'Allah*.

I smiled. "*Insh'Allah*," I repeated.

She smiled back a half-smile, her eyes still holding all her worries. She spoke again, and her husband and daughter both laughed. Safiya translated: "'In the city with the *most* hospitals in the world and the *best* hospitals in the world, nobody can get to the door of *any* hospital.'"

I laughed at a quip so wry that my Jewish grandmother might have also uttered it long ago.

EVERY DAY, IT seemed, different visitors came and went, visitors once from Sudan but now from Washington, D.C., or Toronto or London or Bridgeport or Detroit or L.A. Who would have guessed, so many Sudanese of every hue and tribe, so widely displaced! Who would ever think one man, Ibrahim, would know them all! And each one had a story to tell. I felt, giddily, as if I were immersed in a thousand-and-one nights, the Arabian nights: the endless procession of Arabic-speaking friends from everywhere would prolong his life, story by story, day by day. This feeling was like a drug, and I often went for a fix after work, sitting with the day's assembly for an hour or so in the encampment by the windows which now had chairs, prayer rugs, bags of food and diapers for Karim, the elder man's books with their brittle, yellowing pages, boxes of cookies and cakes, bottles of spring water, toys, fruit juice, sweaters, and slippers. Ibrahim's sister embroidered; his father held a prayer book, unopened. Safiya's brother Mahmoud, a surveyor on leave from a road construction contract in Saudi Arabia, read the previous day's *New York Times* or paced up and down the hallway, impatient but deep in thought, resigned to his family duty here.

One evening another older man was with Ibrahim. Mahmoud whispered to me that this visitor, Gabriel, was a highly respected Dinka and a Catholic. "We have everything," Mahmoud added, smiling. They all knew by now that I was Jewish (or supposed to be). "Hindus, too, next week."

Tall and stately, ebony-skinned and white-haired, frowning, Gabriel withdrew slowly from Ibrahim's room and took the last free chair at the end of the hall, right beside me. We absorbed him wordlessly at first, the usual treatment for the usual reason, as his acute sadness slowly shifted into firm-chinned composure. His grown-up daughters, both from his first marriage to a Canadian, sat cross-legged on the floor: an engineer whose delicate oval face was framed by a mass of unruly curls, and a graduate student of anthropology, square-jawed with intense, light eyes, hair imprisoned in a frizzed ponytail. Both lived in Boston, Safiya told me, introducing one and then the other. "And Gabriel is a great professor of English literature."

He shook my hand. "A professor without profession," he said, a look of irony crossed with bitterness briefly flitting on his face. "In Toronto I have no teaching."

The anthropologist sighed. "You write, Daddy. You write criticism."

He frowned at me. "For more than ten years I have been pre-tending to write criticism, so my children will not pity me."

"Waiting for a Canadian university to offer him a job," said the curly-haired engineer. "But he *does* write. Don't let him pretend he doesn't."

"You can retire now, Daddy. There's no shame in that," said the student.

"Yes, I will feel much better, frittering away my days retired, in-stead of frittering away my days unemployed. Retire from what?"

Both young women laughed and shook their heads.

"Daddy has never had a mind for practicalities. Tell them about your trip here."

He scowled. The elder Dinka with South Sudan etched into his face was beset with smart-aleck American daughters.

The engineer shifted to her knees, settled back on her heels and continued. "We hunt and hunt for a cheap flight for him, and we find one, finally, a real bargain for a hundred dollars if he flies from Buffalo to Providence. So all he has to do is take the bus from Toronto to Buffalo, and then we will drive to Providence to pick him up."

"And what does he do?" cried the other daughter.

Gabriel perked up. "It was too early, this flight from Buffalo." He laughed. "My daughters don't understand an old man's pace. How could I get to the bus station before five in the morning? They say I am not practical, but the only practical thing to do was take a cab."

"To the bus station—was it far?" I asked.

The two young women burst out laughing.

"No," said Gabriel, his eyes suddenly twinkling. "Not to the bus station. To Buffalo. I took the cab to Buffalo."

The engineer frowned. "The cab from Toronto to Buffalo cost more than the round-trip plane ticket."

He shrugged. "My brilliant girls should think a little harder before they connive to move me around on the cheap."

WE WERE ALL packed into Ibrahim's room, the nursing staff scarce, no one hounding us, when Hassan came in. Hassan was an old friend from the family village who had settled in Boston years before Ibrahim and was now the most frequent visitor, the most steadfast helper. But we hadn't seen him for a few days.

"Where have you been?" Safiya asked, frowning. Today she was wearing blue jeans, high heels, a cashmere turtleneck sweater and the more formal two-piece black headscarf. "We have not seen you since—since when? I don't even remember."

"Early last week I was here." He surveyed the room. "But your brother was here, yes? To drive and shop and—"

"We didn't *need* your services. We got around, no problem," she said sternly. Then she broke into a wide smile and swatted him on the arm. "But we missed you."

He smiled a guilty little smile. "I sneaked away."

"You have secrets?" Safiya feigned surprise.

"Of course I have secrets."

"You owe us one."

Hassan laughed. "Okay. I'll tell you one. I was going to tell you one anyway."

"This better be good," said Ibrahim, his voice scratchy.

"It *is* good." Hassan took off his leather jacket, draped it over the back of a chair Ibrahim's father had just brought into the cramped room, and sat down. Immediately Karim climbed up to his lap. Ibrahim's father said something in Arabic, and the others laughed.

"So where were you?" Ibrahim was impatient.

"London," he said, drumming a fast rhythm on Karim's head with both hands. Karim giggled.

"You were in London." Ibrahim sounded skeptical.

Safiya translated for the others, then turned back to Hassan. "Okay, so you were in London."

He held Karim's arms and pushed his hands together into claps. "One, two, three," he said, accompanying each clap. Karim reached for Hassan's beard as he turned to Safiya. "I married Noor in London over the Labor Day break."

Commotion broke out: gasps, cries of surprise, applause, and from Ibrahim's normally silent sister Saleha, a trilling ululation.

"In a long weekend you went to London and you got married? And came back here? What kind of a marriage could that be?" Ibrahim's voice suddenly sounded very strong, very paternal, even though they were not so different in age. He pressed the button to elevate his head so that he was practically sitting up.

Hassan laughed. "The marriage is wonderful. The *wedding* was short and sweet, not so bad. We had two witnesses, the Jamaican couple in the apartment across from Noor's. It took fifteen minutes. A civil wedding, with a judge. Then the five of us had lunch in a Chinese restaurant."

Safiya translated his words to Ibrahim's family. The mother laughed, then spoke, and Safiya translated back.

"Halima says, 'He had to sneak up on his own wedding to make sure it happened this time.'"

Ibrahim sighed, smiling. "They are just such nonconformists, both of them."

Saleha spoke, and Safiya translated. "'How could they go to a Chinese restaurant?' Saleha wants to know."

The mother spoke. Safiya laughed. "'Maybe the judge was Chinese,' she says."

"So this time you married in secret," said Ibrahim, mulling it over.

"Not secret. Just not announced." Hassan shook his head and turned to me. "They will never forget, or let me forget, that I once almost got married but it didn't work out."

Ibrahim explained to me. "You know already, maybe, that Hassan gave up medical school to become a musician. So many instruments, he plays. Noor is an activist for Sudan. She heads a human rights group in exile. Now Hassan does political music when he's not playing with the orchestra. Liberation concerts, he calls them. Benefits. He and Noor, they are both hopeless, beyond help." He winked at Hassan. "A perfect match."

Safiya wrapped her scarf carelessly around her neck. "Asma, the first bride, was absent on the wedding day. A hundred guests had come to the village. And it wasn't easy to get there, believe me. Everyone had arrived, we were already celebrating, but *she* never showed up."

"In Sinja," said Ibrahim, for my benefit. "Where we all came from, back then."

"People stayed another day, until they had finally finished all the food, every last *sanbooksa*," said Safiya. "You think I would forget that?"

"She ran away." Ibrahim frowned. "Asma never came back."

"I inquired. She was okay," said Hassan. "Don't worry about her. She's in Cairo."

"Her family was disgraced."

The elders mumbled in Arabic. Things had turned serious. Hassan replied to them in Arabic. Then everyone was silent.

I broke the silence. "Congratulations to you and Noor, Hassan."

"Thank you very much." He smiled at Ibrahim. "You see? All you have to do is say congratulations."

"Okay, congratulations," whispered Ibrahim.

Safiya burst out with a long response in Arabic, and then they were all laughing and talking in words I didn't understand, while everyone took turns hugging the newlywed.

Ibrahim lowered his bed to recline. "Maybe there was no dancing, but in some ways it is a typical Sudanese marriage these days, with Hassan tied to a job and green card here in Boston, his wife tied to London."

"At least it's only one continent away," I said.

"She is looking for a job here," said Hassan. "Eventually she will move here to America."

"And then you will have the *real* wedding, yes? The big one?" asked Safiya.

"Yes, with family and friends."

"Good." Ibrahim sighed, took off his glasses and closed his eyes. "Good," he murmured softly. He pulled the blanket up to his chin. Color had drained from his face. He looked ancient, suddenly. "Tell Noor, please, that I'm sorry I won't be able to attend."

A DAY IN late September, the world now turned upside down, Ibrahim took my hand after the others had left together to have lunch in the hospital cafeteria.

"How are you doing, Professor Erika?" he asked. "You look so sad."

I shrugged. "I can't pretend to be feeling good."

"You suffer for what the world does. The world's agonies become your personal problems, yes?"

I laughed a forced laugh. "Is that what it is? I don't know. Early last week, Abby, my colleague—she was one of your teachers, wasn't she? Abby asked me how I was. I told her I was depressed, and she asked why. *Why?* I said, well, New York was attacked, three thousand people were slaughtered, and the president's men have put us all in lockdown, like a state of siege. And she said, in all seriousness, 'Oh, can we still use 9/11 as an excuse?'"

He laughed deeply, and I laughed for real this time.

"Not even a month later, we're supposed to be over it."

We sat silently for a minute. Then he said, "So much senseless violence. Everywhere. And will they declare a war now?"

"Probably. To add more senseless violence."

He sighed. "And who is it who gets to decide which senseless violence is more senseless, more wicked, or more dangerous than the other senseless violence? In my country, hundreds, thousands of children die from malaria. Isn't that also senseless violence?"

"People shoot each other on the streets of Boston."

"All over America they shoot each other; they even shoot themselves," he whispered, closing his eyes. "Everywhere." For a minute he was silent. Then he spoke again. "We rush death, as if it is not already overtaking us as fast as it can." He looked down at his own emaciated chest. "We say life is a precious gift, we say life is sacred, but look at this self-destructive impulse of humanity, the way it throws itself toward extinction." We frowned at one another. "And you, you are home alone getting sadder?" He asked sternly.

"I have friends nearby. I have phone calls with family, I am at work all day with people."

"That is still too alone, at a time of crisis it is not good for you to be so much by yourself. To be so available for the general grief."

"But I'm here. How could I be so alone if I'm *here*?"

He sighed. "I mean no children, no husband. Why is that? You'll forgive me for prying? I am not too rude?"

Now I sighed. "No, you are never too rude. Sometimes I can pass for normal, and you may *think* I am a regular professor like the others, but really I am very weird. Odd."

He laughed. "You are *not* weird. You are different, but not weird."

Today, I now understood, the Arabian night was *me*.

"Okay. Here's the short version. I was married to an artist, a sculptor. The marriage died out slowly. There was no tragedy, but after twelve years we weren't happy. The spark was long gone. We got divorced."

Ibrahim's scowl deepened. "Simple as that? The spark was gone so you divorced?"

"Yes, almost as simple as that. You know divorce is easy, it happens here all the time, in the States. And I didn't want kids. I knew what having kids was like because everyone else had them. The world didn't need me to have them, too, did it? I yearned for a life less predictable, riskier."

"You wanted to take risks." He seemed to mull it over.

I laughed. "But what did I really do? Okay, I traveled, I juggled funny jobs in funny places, I wrote. For many years I fought off this stability, this academic career in which you found me, but I didn't become a war correspondent or mountain climber or deep-sea diver; I was never a barefoot doctor or a freedom fighter. I've taken no big risks. Except to have no children—that was the biggest risk, I suppose. Funny, huh?"

He shook his head. "Do you see me laughing?"

"But Ibrahim, I have no regrets."

His eyebrows arched. "Really?"

"Really. And you see how I love my friends' children."

He squeezed my hand. "Maybe your students are your children. *Old* children, like me."

"Maybe."

"Your pages of writing, they are your children, too, yes?"

"Yes."

We sat in silence for a few minutes, just holding hands. He closed his eyes. Then he opened them. "We will have to leave soon, you know. We will have to return to Abu Dhabi."

"But no!"

"The atmosphere here is not good. Safiya cannot wear her *hijab* on the street without getting hostile looks. My mother and sister, with their chador, only come straight here, but they are even feeling the hostility when they walk through the hospital. Right now in the cafeteria, who knows what's happening? How many stares and frowns must they pretend not to see? How many insults, spoken or not? It is too hard for them."

I looked down at the floor, ashamed.

"Really, now I am the only one in the family who feels safe, because I am lying here in what they call a johnnie." He laughed softly. "Not even a prayer rug, to remind the doctors and nurses I'm a Muslim, an Arab."

I realized he probably had not walked to the end of the hall; he may not have known of the family's encampment, how the hospital marveled at such a Bedouin display.

"It's wrong, this nationalism. This intolerant backlash," I said.

He shrugged. "It's a Christian country."

"But it's not! It's everything! Look at me!"

"But you are not a very good Jew." He knew I had no religious beliefs, that I observed no holidays at all. I smiled. He smiled. "In fact you are a terrible Jew."

"But if I wanted to practice, nothing would stop me."

"Yes, you are free to practice. But I think they are almost as hostile to your kind of practitioners as they are to us. I think the fundamentalist Christians are very much like the extreme Muslims who just attacked."

I shook my head, agreeing. "That self-righteousness crops up in all fundamentalist sects, Orthodox Jews, too, of course."

Ibrahim sighed. "Anyone who disagrees with extremists of any faith, with their one and only right way, is an outcast. An enemy."

"And they want their women to stay home having children and obeying. Putting women in their place always seems to be part of *any* extremism. The Taliban have no monopoly on *that*."

"So you and I, a so-so Muslim and a so-called Jew, we agree." He squeezed my hand again. "But your president talks of crusades, of holy war. Even though Muslims living here are as outraged and grief-stricken about the attacks as anyone else, we have been targeted." He pointed high up to his television set. "I know what's going on."

Again my face burned with shame. "But you also know we are not *all* like that."

"But it's the ones who *are* like that who control things, who hold all the power."

"Ibrahim," I said sternly, "believe me, your family will be okay here. Everyone will be okay. *You* don't have to leave."

His mouth twitched into a grin. "You are sounding like my teacher again."

"You're getting the very best care here, right?"

"Yes, Professor."

"Everyone is able to come to you here, yes?"

"Yes, Professor."

I paid no heed to his mischievous smile. "*Please* don't leave."

He sighed. "We shall see."

Seven

❖

You'd think she'd know better. She wanted her life back, she wanted her world back. She bought albums and dug up the boxes of photographs stashed in closets. She dumped the boxes out onto the living room floor, hundreds of snapshots all jumbled together—her five-year-old self on the backyard swing set, a plane refueling in Rekyevik on her first trip to Europe, a former student's children feeding ostriches in Nairobi just last year. Surely she could make better sense of herself, when the rest of the world made no sense now. What a simpleton she'd become! First she sorted the photos into piles on the rug: her childhood, her parents and sister at all ages, her studies abroad, college friends, adult friends, cousins and aunts and uncles, pals at jobs, boyfriends, her lives in this place and that and the other, her gardens, offices, friends' children, the usual banalities of existence. Of that sort of existence. (Everyone should be so lucky.) By the end of that first weekend, eleven piles were arranged on the living room floor, ready to reconstitute the world she'd once known. Monday evening she sorted through one pile and mounted the photographs of her childhood, and Tuesday she went through the most recent couple of years, filling a second album. Order! But the more she tried to make sense of the years in between, the more they splintered, overlapped, refused categories or timelines. The following week, she stepped around the remaining piles. And after that she gathered up the loose photos and threw them into boxes again, returning them to closet shelves. It was too late to impose an order on life. That had to be true long before any towers fell.

IVAN AND I make it a day trip in October, Columbus Day weekend, leaving very early in the morning for Cape Cod, for Nauset beach. Finally we are going to a *real* beach, not the pebbly little crescent of sand down the street from my house, with its view of the Boston skyline, the drone of planes overhead, and its timid waters. No, today we have headed for open seas, pounding surf, miles of sparkly, untainted coast. The day is warm, breezy, and sunny. First we take a long walk barefoot on the wet low-tide sand, going well past the houses perched up on the dunes. Gazing out to sea, we detect the shiny round head of a gray seal offshore, and then another, and then a multitude of seals swimming along the shoreline, diving and resurfacing, at play. It seems too early in the season for seals, but there they are. They follow us with their eyes, grinning at us as they stop in one place exactly when we stand in one place, grinning out to them. They watch us, smiling. I walk into icy water up to my knees; waves roll in, break where I don't expect them to and splash me hard. I jump and holler. Ivan laughs at me. The seals laugh at me. Even I laugh at me. I'm drenched, my shorts are soaked, but I don't care. Brilliant sunlight reflects in dapples on the seals and on the waves, which ripple gently to the beach. Today there are no crashing breakers. Ducks ride the current, unfluttered.

After the walk, we set up our little beach chairs in an empty spot a few hundred yards from the path to the parking lot, out of earshot of other people. Ivan spreads out a small red-and-white checked blanket, opens a picnic cooler, unfolds two red linen napkins for place settings. He knows how to do this just right. A small bottle of champagne is still buried in ice.

"Alcohol isn't allowed on the beach," I say.

"Then we'll have to get rid of it." Ivan takes the bottle from its frozen bed, pops the cork and raises his first pouring for a toast. "To lazy days on the beach, and absence of terror." We clink glasses and drink.

The sandwiches are European perfection, with mozzarella, prosciutto, and ripe tomatoes on a crusty baguette in the first one we share, then goat cheese and spring greens in another. We go slowly. By the time we get to the second sandwich, we have finished the champagne and move on to a mellow Côte du Rhône. For dessert, Ivan pulls his ancient Swiss Army knife from a pocket and quarters two peaches, now warm from the sun.

We set the backs of our chairs at lower angles. We each take a book from a knapsack. I put on my big floppy straw hat, while Ivan tucks a napkin into the back of his cap in the style of Lawrence of Arabia. He leans back, opens the book on his lap, and stretches his feet deep into the sand, burying his gnarled toes. His tee shirt rides up, revealing the little black curls around his navel and the steep slope of his middle paunch; he is altogether unselfconscious, his clothes rumpled, his hair windblown, the grains of sand in it catching the light. Together, like an old couple in a well-rehearsed ritual, as if we are anchored securely in ordinary life and the world is predictable and safe, we sit there together reading, wordless, dozing off in the sun, rousing, reading, sipping drinks, dozing again. Even as the sun makes its inevitable descent, the precious afternoon lingers for us, outside time.

I awake, shivering, to voices. A cloud is passing across the sun, now very pale and low in the sky, and the air is cold. The waves are

slapping on the sand with more force than before, leaving thick scal-
loped trails of bubbly foam only a few yards from our feet. The tide
has come in. Ivan is alert, perched forward in his chair. Gathered
about a hundred feet away is a group of people peering toward a
central focus on the sand. Theirs are the voices I've heard.

"There's a seal on the beach," says Ivan. "I saw it haul out
there on its belly. Like it was just coming up for a change of scenery
or to hang out with us. He didn't seem hurt or anything. And now
he's cornered."

"I got the camera!" a kid shrieks, running to a man in long,
baggy shorts. Another man is already stepping closer and closer
to the seal with video camera in hand. A large woman in a billowing tunic shoots pictures with a cell phone. I realize that people in
a closed ring around the seal block any possible escape, shouting,
gawking, kicking up sand, harassing it.

"Shit," I say. "They come all this way to a National Park filled
with wildlife. And then they fuck around with it."

Ivan calls out, "Hey people, why don't you leave it alone. Back
off. Let it get away." His voice has the soft pleading tone he might
use after his students screw up an exam.

A couple of the people turn and stare at him, but no one replies
and no one backs away. Several move even closer to the seal, which
rocks on its belly, making a mournful cry.

Ivan gets up and walks to the crowd. I see him gesticulating,
pointing this way and that. I hear them laughing to one another
behind his back. I see him demonstrating how to move to a reason-
able distance. He stands away from them, pointing down at his
feet. Some of them stare at him, while the kids all take one more

deliberate step closer to the seal, which has stopped rocking. No parent intervenes. He shrugs. I hear the final word he calls out to them: *respect.*

He returns to me with tears in his eyes. "Americans!" he says bitterly. "No offense to you, but they can't leave well enough alone." He abruptly begins to pack up our blanket and napkins, our wine glasses and trash and plates; he takes off his hat and packs that in, too. Together we put away the books and fold up the chairs, then traipse back through the sand and up the fenced dune to the car.

On the drive to Boston, we listen to the radio, the news, the re-play of the president's midday announcement, which we'd missed, of the first bombing of Afghanistan. The movement of troops and materiel, the glory of his mission.

"Nothing like a good war to end the violence," says Ivan. "That always works, doesn't it?"

"Americans," I say. And then we are quiet all the long way home.

I HAVE READ again, caught up online, so this I know: Mr. Edwards is out of prison; he has been out now for three or four years, let go for good behavior. The family of the victim was not happy, but in judicial circles nobody seemed to mind. Not long after his original wife divorced him, another woman entered the picture and mar-ried him while he was still doing time, one of those women whose compassion and passion are stirred by locked-up men who've com-mitted unspeakable acts and can only be seen in short visits. But even this wife has left him, too, I've read. She must be in love again with another prisoner now, preferring her men remain behind bars.

Once a man is in her home, sitting around in his undershirts and varicose veins, the glow must wear off fast. Mr. Edwards's daughters of course will never speak to him again, they have renounced all contact, even the name. I am sure. He doesn't blame them. But eventually he feels compelled to get reacquainted with his only son. I think.

One morning as I come back from the library I see a man on campus just hanging around: large, more than heavyset, a man who has grown obese. Or *is* he just hanging around? I follow him across the quad. He is oh so slow, so plodding. But then his slow, elephantine march begins to look more deliberate for a few yards. Maybe he is just passing through. But no, he plops down on a bench not far from our building. He stares off into space, unfazed by the cold air, unblinking in the late winter sun, his face a blank. He is too well dressed to be homeless, but he is not dressed well enough to belong professionally somewhere in the medical school. Perhaps he is a patient. Perhaps he comes here for treatment at the mental health clinic just beyond the other side of the quad. Maybe regular psychiatric therapy was a condition of his early release. Maybe he doesn't even know his son works on this very same campus. But maybe he does. Oh yes, he knows. I think he's waiting. He wants to go into the building but doesn't dare. Not yet. So he lurks. This is not the first time he has lurked here, oh no. This is a well-rehearsed routine. He wants to catch a glimpse of Toby. He is far too preoccupied with spying on his son to realize that someone he once knew is right behind, spying on *him*. He would never remember me, and even if he did he would never recognize me nearly forty years later! If he recalled anything at all, it would be the long, thin face of a slightly precocious, slightly myopic adolescent wearing her sister's ugly hand-me-downs. But he will not recall. He has not seen *my* picture in the paper like I've seen his in the intervening years as he became older, fatter, obsessed, and dazed—not fully baked and yet stale at the same time. But the photographs from the arrest and the trial were many years ago. He must have changed since then, too. So I'm not really sure this is him, lurking on the quad, and I can't get a good look at his face. It's too creepy; it's so unlikely; probably it's not him.

I head back to my office. Definitely it's not him. Of course it's unlikely to be him. The odds are against it.

But the man-in-the-flesh, whoever he is, has caught me off-guard. Maybe it really *is* him.

WHEN I GOT to the end of the hospital hallway, Ibrahim's friend Gabriel, the elder Dinka from Canada, was deep in conversation with two very tall, very thin, very young men. "It is not Africa anymore," he was saying. "Forget the tribe. You have to think about yourselves now. Dinka, Nuer, Lotuka—it doesn't matter. In America, nobody cares. Individualism is what counts here. Not the tribe. You cannot be afraid to be alone."

Gabriel introduced me to them, Niel and Deng. They stood up.

"We are Lost Boys of Sudan," Niel said, towering over me as we shook hands.

"Welcome. I know a little of your story, and how you spent years walking to get to a refugee camp. I am very happy you are here, and very happy to meet you."

"Thank you so much," they said in unison, shaking my hand again. Then they sat down.

"Now we go to high school in Watertown. So we are even more lost," said Deng, who I'd noticed was even taller than the other. They both laughed in a high-pitched tone.

Gabriel smiled at me. "Ibrahim has been taken away for a scan, so we are idling here until he comes back. Please idle with us." He turned to the young men again, his face becoming stern. "To be an individual, meet your own potential, get an education, make your mark on the world, that is the goal here. *That's* how you will help your people in Sudan. Believe me, there is no other way."

"But we have to find whoever is left in our families at home. Or maybe we will find them in Kakuma camp now."

"And when we find them, we have to send them money. Think how bad off they are there. Now we can work and support them."

"No," said Gabriel. "No. Listen to me carefully. You cannot spend your time and energy worrying about them. You know they will do what they have to do to survive, just like you did. And you will have to work very hard just to make your way in this new world, which is already hard enough. Your debt to your families and your tribe is to become the very best you can become here, yourself; to get a good education. Not to be obsessed with them. Not to send them your money."

"That's very harsh," I said quietly.

"Yes, it is the harsh truth."

The young men let a silent minute pass, then Niel, the not-quite-as-tall Lost Boy, spoke up. "It is strange that *you* are telling us that. You have never forgotten where you came from."

"But I myself had to make the changes long ago. That's exactly why I say these things."

"But you did not leave because soldiers attacked your home and family. Your village was not burned, your parents were not killed. You had choices. And you left by choice."

Gabriel laughed gruffly. "Once I became educated, I did not have so many choices. I know, we tell you it is the other way around. It should be. And for you, getting an education here, it will be. Doors will open, even as others may have closed. Doors you have never dreamed of. But back then I was a stranger in my own society. The intellectual work I was trained to do I could not do at home. You may not have chosen exile, but you are also strangers in Sudan now."

They listened but looked at him skeptically. "But you still know the traditions, the culture."

"I know them but I do not *do* them. I treasure the stories, but I do not live my life by them. I have no cattle. I paid no cattle as a bride price. There is no such thing as pure culture. It has to change along with times and circumstances. It is not only you who changed because you came here. Tradition has changed, too, even back there. It was traditional for girls to be married at ten or twelve years of age and never to be educated. We are happy to change the culture so that our girls have a chance to fulfill themselves."

"Here we have no choice now but to learn and change," said Deng. "But what we change is *things*, what we have and what we do. Not who we *are*. It is not our souls that change."

Gabriel smiled at me. "They had to learn how to flush a toilet. How to turn on an electric light switch."

Both of these tall men who were still boys, or boys who were already men, giggled without inhibition. Niel said, "The electric ice. That is truly wonderful. Now we drink cold milk and cold soda.

We play soccer with our classmates. We do homework. We have after-school jobs."

Deng's expression became serious as he looked into my face. "We try to go out with white girls, but they say no. We don't know why. What is wrong with us?"

"Nothing!" I cried. "You may think you needed to catch up with so much in the modern West, but the teenage girls here in your school must be so terribly immature, so very childish compared to you, after all you have been through."

They giggled again and seized on the opening I had made for them. "The American girls worry about their clothes and shopping. There is always food in their houses, and all they have to do is put things in the microwave. They have no worries at all, but they don't know it."

"But our Sudanese girls, the girls who are Lost Boys, are not sure they can go to the movies with us. So they don't. They are afraid it will mean we are getting married."

"We can't marry yet. We have no cattle," said Deng.

"There you go again," muttered Gabriel. "Cattle!"

I was confused. "How can girls be Lost Boys?"

"Because your newspapers and even the churches that brought us here called all of us Lost Boys, but there were always some girls. Only a very few sometimes."

Suddenly we were hushed by the metallic clanging of a gurney being pushed down the hallway from the elevator. We watched Ibrahim and his helper draw near.

Ibrahim opened his eyes and smiled when he saw us. "You slackers!" he called out, rolling by and into the room. We all followed.

ONE DAY LATER that week, two very tall, very thin young women were talking with Safiya and Ibrahim and his mother in his room.

"You wanted to meet these girls," Safiya said to me.

"We are Lost Boys," they said in unison, eyes twinkling. They both had beautiful smiles, flashing astoundingly big, even, white teeth.

Ibrahim said, "No, you are found girls."

"You were never lost," I said, as we all shook hands. "Were you?"

"That's right." Grace, the older girl, spoke with quiet dignity. "We did not always know where we were. For months we walked and hid from soldiers and swam across rivers and covered ourselves with grasses to hide from men and the sun. But we knew where we wanted to be. We followed where others had gone to be safe. So we were not ever lost."

"Until we got here," added Rachael.

"Tell Professor Erika about your American families," said Ibrahim. He took my hand. "She is an American, too. We will hold her responsible for all of them." He kept my hand in his.

"When our American families catch us looking sad, they make us feel we are ungrateful. But we are very grateful. That has nothing to do with being sad. They don't understand what happened before."

"If we try to explain, they start to talk about something else."

"My father was killed," whispered Rachael. She cleared her throat and continued in a stronger voice. "I was separated from my mother and brothers and sisters and I don't know if any of them are alive now. I saw soldiers shoot my friends as they tried to swim across a river. I saw other friends drown in the river because they couldn't swim, and others collapse under the hot sun. How can I not be sad sometimes?"

"It is amazing if you are not sad *all* the time," I said.

"When we visit our other friends from Sudan, the families tell us we are refusing to adjust."

"They are angry if we are late for anything." Both girls laughed.

"We are not accustomed to looking at clocks. It is not even polite for us to come at the time someone says, even if we know what the time is."

A moment of silence passed.

"They are always asking what they can buy for us." The two girls laughed again.

"They give us more and more, and we don't need more and more. We just want to be with our own friends from Sudan sometimes."

"Of course," I said. I didn't know what else to do. I hugged them. Then we kept talking until the nurse chased us out of Ibrahim's room.

Eight

❖

There was no real defense, even all the war years after. Bungling arrogance, but no defense. Lots of money changing hands, contractors getting rich, you might even call it profiteering, war profiteering, you might even call it a war made expressly for profiteers, but there was no true defense. You run through it all again now, knowing now what you know now, superimposed on what you felt then, feared then, suspected then, and it's even worse. Try it.

"THE DICHOTOMY OF interpretation remains ambiguous." Over and over again I read the six-word sentence which halts me like a barbed wire fence in the middle of Alice's problem statement. She is on her sixth topic. Child trafficking in Nepal was the first. Female genital mutilation in Somalia came next. Gender-related violence in complex humanitarian emergencies settled in for several weeks, then the health consequences of illiteracy among women. I personally liked microbicides and female condoms: can women take control and find the way out of AIDS? But that topic didn't stick, either. There are just so many dreadful, unjust things happening in the world, making for so many irresistible topics. Alice is the proverbial child in the candy store: which one will she pick? This time, it's the need for male involvement in family planning. But I don't get it when she says that the dichotomy of interpretation remains ambiguous.

Maybe what I experience here as I read these words, this opaqueness, this stultifying bewilderment that feels like someone has poured wet cement into the interstices of my brain which is now quickly hardening into concrete, maybe this sensation is precisely what the sentence means. I wonder.

Somebody clears his throat in my doorway. "There's popcorn," Toby says. I look up from the mystifying sentence to the meaningless grin on his round face. He is the human smiley-face. I hadn't noticed before how he's gaining weight, but now I see it. "There's popcorn in the kitchen all set to go if anybody wants it. I made popcorn."

"Thanks, Toby." I look back at the paper, but sense the space in my doorway remains occupied.

"We got the grant," he says.

"Huh?" I am forced to look up at him again.

"You know, the Nairobi study."

"Oh, good."

"Good to go for four more years. The NIH likes it. Naturally *they* understand why there can't be an intervention before the full four years."

He lingers there, inert, blocking my doorway. On the exterior he is all pudginess, padded in layers of adult baby-fat, while something in his very core—maybe the very core itself—seems to be missing. Where other people carry their selves, their essentials, Toby has a hollow space, an unfilled pit excavated by his father's ax.

"*They* understand," he says again. "At the NIH."

What does he want from me? To fill that pit inside? Hey, not me. I can't. I won't.

"That's great, Toby." I look at his blank face, the dullness of his eyes. A shadow of his former self, I think. But no, not his own self. The shadow of a different self. "Do you—"

The question tries to push out onto my lips: Do you ever see *your father*? But I don't let it. I'm afraid. What if he turns the family rage on *me*? What if I unleash all that's been bubbling right beneath the surface?

"What?" he asks. His voice is calm. Maybe there *is* no rage. Maybe rage is not hereditary. Maybe there is no genetic predisposition to cutting women up in pieces after all. That would be nice. But how do I know?

"Never mind," I say.

"Better hurry before it's all gone," he says.

"What?"

"The popcorn." Finally he leaves.

I fix my eyes on Alice's page again, and force myself past the ambiguity of interpretation's dichotomy.

IN THE MORNING, in bed after we've again made what has become our quiet, unspectacular but satisfying love, condom-free, and he is holding me, snuggled up behind, Ivan says, "Anya is coming tomorrow. She has a vacation and she'll be here for two weeks."

"Anya is coming *tomorrow*? For *two weeks*? And you're telling me *now*?"

He squeezes me affectionately. "You always knew about Anya. I talk about Anya all the time. I don't hide anything."

This is true. It sounds too much to me like a well-rehearsed reminder, one that has perhaps been uttered in many beds, getting him off many a hook, but it is true. And whenever he is speaking on the phone in Russian, which is very often, in his office or at home, even once or twice on his cell phone at *my* place, I assume he is talking with Anya. I have never asked questions, but he never tries to hide. Then again, he is speaking in Russian and knows I don't understand. How convenient, to have women not only on different continents, but in different languages.

"Does she know about *me?*" I pull away from him and roll over on my back.

He doesn't answer.

"No, of course not." I answer my own question. "You've never told her about me." The situation is not just now starting, but it becomes more real, now that she's on her way.

He leans over and kisses me. I don't kiss back. He says, "She knows you are a friend and colleague. I've never told her we sleep together."

"She knows you have friends and colleagues. I happen to be one of them. Do I have a name?"

He sits up, swings his legs sideways off the bed.

"Do I even have a name? If you introduced us, would she say, 'Oh yes, Erika, Ivan has often spoken of you'?" I don't know why it matters, that she should know about me specifically. Maybe it's best that she doesn't; maybe what we have is too serious for him to talk about with her at this point. Momentarily that's a cheering thought. But I can't let go. Two weeks!

Elbows on his knees, he holds his head in his hands.

"Should I invite the two of you over to my place for dinner? Like a good friend and colleague?"

He doesn't reply. He sits there naked on the edge of the bed, holding his head in his hands and staring out the window, at the weathered gray shingles of the house next door to his. I lie there naked in the steamy afterglow of sarcasm. We are naked and silent together for a few minutes. Then suddenly he stands up and ducks into the shower.

The sound of water running at full speed will drown me out.

"And *now* you tell me? She's coming *tomorrow*? For *two weeks*?" He can't possibly hear me.

Why am I making a scene? It is, after all, only an ambivalent, half-hearted little scene. It's true that his announcement hurts like a knife in the gut, but a dull knife, a small knife, a kid's penknife, piercing no deeper than the top layer of my belly adipose. It's his passivity that really galls me, not his two-timing. Perhaps they amount to the same thing: a reluctance to decide or choose. But I don't really want to be chosen. No. I have easily, maybe too easily, accepted the limits to our affair; in fact, I'd probably prefer things this way, if only the terrorists weren't winning. I don't want to have to tell him to get his hair cut, to remember his son's birthday or his grandson's, to stop using so much salt or drinking so much wine. I'd just as soon let Anya have the nagging. She can also have the pot belly, the endless rounds of periodontal surgery, the bald spot that's just starting to show and all the laments of self-pity that erupt each time he notices it. Beautiful young Anya can push his wheel-chair when the time comes, too. Maybe I'm like those women who marry prisoners: generally I do not want a full-time man. Generally

97

I am happy alone, except when the world is coming to an end and nobody else seems to notice. Except Ivan.

But the timing offends me: why did he wait until almost the last minute? On the off chance we are blown to smithereens before she arrives and he need not have incurred my irritation at all?

Why did he tell me in bed, when we were wrapped around one another? So that I might feel secure in his affections, despite being dumped for two weeks?

I get stiffly out of bed and throw on his robe. A Halloween season chill nips through this house. We will talk about these things later, maybe, when, after two weeks, we resume. If we resume.

THE PROFESSORS HAMID from Providence, husband and wife, economist and sociologist, were almost out the door when I got to Ibrahim's hospital room one evening. Ibrahim introduced us. The man professor, wearing a gray suit, was extremely tall and thin, while the woman professor, in sweater and fashionably long skirt, head uncovered, was tiny. We said our greetings, my head bobbing up and down from one smiling face to the other, and then they left to join the family at the encampment. I would be going there, too, but Ibrahim gestured for me to sit beside the bed, the seat of honor.

He sighed, then spoke hoarsely. "All these people from Sudan have green cards. You see how they start over, once they're here, and live their lives. But don't be fooled. The assimilation is only cosmetic. They would go back in half a second, if things changed in Khartoum and if peace came to the South."

"But meanwhile they all come to see you."

He worked the dial of the morphine contraption. "Soon I will dope myself up so much, it will make no difference if I am here or not. They will be talking only to each other."

"You have to be as comfortable as possible."

He laughed. "Only in America do you think of dying as a comfortable activity."

"I'm sorry," I said.

He reached out and weakly squeezed my hand. "When my blood count gets a little better"—he gestured to a liquid dripping into his intravenous line, a drug meant to bring about this one reprieve—"we will go back to Abu Dhabi, the whole family and me."

A chill ran up my spine. This time I understood that he was absolutely serious. What would I do when he left? When they all left? He may have been dying, but at least he was dying *here*.

"I want to be with all the children. I want to be as lucid as I possibly can. I have to see them go to school every morning. Until—" He stopped, but I rushed to keep the silent spot from becoming the unsaid words.

"Yes, of course," I said, my stomach dropping. "I understand."

IT'S EARLY IN the morning, too early to start reading about insecticide-treated bednets for malaria prevention, the first topic in the pile of outlines on my desk. I flip through the others. Guinea worm eradication in Togo. Preventing HIV among intravenous drug users in Kazakhstan. Maternal mortality in Indonesia. Drug pricing and the World Trade Organization. None of the topics strike me as an especially auspicious way to start the day.

"There's banana cake in the kitchen." Toby is standing in my doorway again, round-faced and round-shouldered and in every possible way rounder than he was before. Becoming, in fact, as round as Mr. Edwards was, back when. Lately he comes and talks when we are the only ones here in the morning. He's holding the mug with the big smiley-face on it and takes a slurp. "Coffee's good to go, too." I am trying hard not to see an ax instead of a mug. "The banana cake has a surprise. Chocolate chips. My wife makes it like that."

"That was nice of her, Toby, to send us a cake." A surprise in the Edwards cake: razor blades. Thumb tacks. Arsenic. Battery acid.

"Tina's a great cook." He chuckles, then puts a hand on his round abdomen.

"Yeah, you better watch out, Toby. We *all* better watch out." Since Toby started working here, the department is booby-trapped with calories and cholesterol. I look back down at the pages on my desk.

"Hey, y'know the orphan project in Kenya? The proposal I wrote?"

I sigh. "Yeah. I know the one. Actually, *we* wrote it. Together. You and I."

He disregards my point. "I just got an email from Frances. It took a turn south. One of the local staff screwed up big-time." He has a wide grin across his face, almost as if he's happy about this turn of events.

"What happened?"

He laughs. "She *intervened.*"

"Yeah?" Good for her, I say to myself.

"She was the data collector, the one who interviewed all the household members at certain intervals. She spoke Kikuyu and Swahili and she could go into all the neighborhoods. We thought she was pretty good. The work got done, and it got done on time. But then she like totally blew it." His round face still wears a self-satisfied smiley-face grin, but he makes the gesture of cutting his throat with his forefinger. It takes my breath away, this gesture. He slices his own throat with his father's ax, right before my eyes.

I eventually summon words. "What did she do?"

"She gave them money. She gave money and stuff to the households. We're supposed to be measuring like how much they've got and what they do with it and what they've got left after that, and if the kids gain weight or start wasting, and what does she go and do? Shit. She *gives* them stuff. Frances is bouncing off the walls. Nussbaum doesn't even know about it yet. I heard about it first." He grins. It's important to him, that he has the scoop. The first step in out-Nussbauming Nussbaum. "He'll hit the roof."

"Where did she get the money?" I am curious, but he is not.

"Who knows." He shrugs.

"What else did she give them? Food? Medicine?"

He shrugs again. "Beats me. All I know is she's outta there. Frances gave her the boot the minute she caught on. And now we have to figure out if the project is totally wrecked. Like if it's beyond the point of no return. Or if we need to hire a replacement to pick up the pieces and glue them back together. Maybe they'll want me to go over there."

"That's too bad."

He grins. "I upgraded my trouble-shooting toolkit in a special training on my last job. So maybe I can salvage things, if I can see for myself. I know all the stakeholders, but there's a limit to how much back-stopping we can do from here. We need a solid skill set on the ground. Someone who can prioritize."

The buzzwords make my head buzz.

"And actually I wouldn't mind making the trip over there. I wouldn't even mind staying for a while."

I sigh, deflecting a shudder. "Frances is the principal investigator, right?"

"Yeah. But she's not really an admin type. She's a researcher type. She doesn't have a head for management, like I do. She wasn't keeping an eye on things. Too fixated on the data. Not paying enough attention to the deliverables. Wrong skill set."

"So you would straighten that out?"

"Yeah. She has this thing about hiring local people. But maybe that's not such a good idea. I mean, maybe it's okay to have a local driver, or a translator, but for the really important stuff, watch out. Made in USA is what I say."

I lean back in my chair and take a big breath. "Toby, you've never worked on an international project before, have you? Some people would say that projects should be staffed *only* by local people. Did that idea ever occur to you?"

"Yeah. But look what happened with just *one*," he says. The grin is gone. He stares at me and keeps staring, as if the longer he holds me in his sights, the more permanently and incontrovertibly the point he's making will sink in and stay.

"That's exactly what I'm driving at, Toby. There was only *one*. Can you generalize from a sample of *one*?"

"I'm not talking about statistics," he says. "I'm talking about management. Skill. *Control*." His stare gets icier, the set of his jaw hardens.

I resist the shudder that's starting up in my spine. Can *I* generalize from a sample of one? A sample of one Edwards?

"Okay," I say. "Good luck." Suddenly insecticide-treated bed-nets and junkies with AIDS in Kazakhstan are looking pretty good. I cast my own stare back down at the outlines.

But what I see is not junkies in Kazakhstan. I see a little boy forced to take the stand, mute, at his own father's murder trial. Oh shit. Toby, ten years old. Round bodied, undeveloped button nose, colorless crew cut. He sits stiffly at the front of the courtroom facing everyone, his heart thumping in his chest. He is more alone than he has ever been before. His mother stares down into her lap, his sisters look up into the air at some nonexistent point off in the distance. Everyone abandons him. Even sound abandons him. He sees things that would make noise—a court official in a dark blue uniform opens and closes a door, an attorney coughs into his fist, people whisper in the rows—but he hears nothing. A thick, impenetrable quiet descends upon him, upon the room, upon the world. This is the silence that will forever stand between Toby and the rest of his life.

"You reading papers again?" he asks me, still in the doorway.

"Yeah. Mostly just outlines. Problem statements."

I don't look, but he lingers for a few more moments, watching me read, I can tell. I hear the elevator open on our floor, the voices of other people getting out. I try not to be relieved at this, knowing we are no longer alone up here, with him staring at me from the doorway, but I *am* relieved. I breathe an actual sigh of relief, now that other people are on the floor.

He says, "There's banana cake. Don't forget. It'll be gone before you know it."

"Send Tina my thanks," I say with false heartiness, still not looking up. "Bye-bye, Toby."

"Bye. Have a great day."

I watch him turn away from my doorway and begin the march down the hall to his own office. But I also see an aging prosecutor who bends down and leans in toward a child who sees, too close, the man's chapped lips press and open, jaws pump up and down, silver fillings sparkle in gigantic molars, liver-spotted cheeks stretch in insincere smiles. Toby smells the mouth's fetid breath. He hears nothing.

He is not supposed to talk. He will not talk. He is on the stand for less than four minutes and says nothing.

Beating faster and faster, his heart thumps not with noise but with fists hammering on the inside of his chest. He grasps the sides of the chair to hold himself steady, to keep from slipping and sliding with the earthquake in his heart. He looks to the right; his father grins at him and for a split second the pounding stops; then, when he can't bear his father's face and looks away, it comes back, doubly strong. He tries it again: he looks at his father. His father grins. The pounding skips two beats until Toby fixes his eyes on his own knees. *Thud*-thud. *Thud*-thud. *Thud*-thud. *Thud*-thud.

He tries to think himself away from the pounding and focuses on his collar. It is too stiff, too new. Where it stands straight up from the V of his yellow pullover, it pokes into his neck and chin. How he fought with his mother that morning, to not wear a tie. And he won. He wears no tie. And yet the collar itself is an unyielding slab and chokes him. At another end of himself he feels the bunchy folds where one sock has slinked down into the heel of his left loafer. Meanwhile, a long, twisty growl snakes across his stomach. He moves one hand to clutch the soft cushion of his midsection through the pullover, as if he could grab the rumble inside and stop it. Then an itch takes up residence like a flying insect on the tip of his nose, but he is sure he shouldn't scratch it when everyone is looking. For a very long minute, he is consumed with the urgency to reach up to his nose; nothing else exists except the hammering in his chest and the tormenting itch and the will to keep his hand from springing up to touch it. He wiggles his nose. It itches more. He sniffs in. He sniffs out. He sniffs in again. Now he's going to sneeze. That should do it. He holds his breath, waiting for the sneeze, feeling the nose itch inside and outside, waiting to sneeze, quaking with the *thud*-thud, *thud*-thud, *thud*-thud. The nose begins twitching without him but the sneeze doesn't come, everything is all blocked up in there, and yet the twitching tip of his nose escapes from him, the itch rides bareback on the bucking bronco nose.

The first time someone says, "You can step down now, Toby," he doesn't hear it. The next time, a hand touches his shoulder, not pressing hard, yet not particularly gentle. He gets up from the chair. His older sister catches his eye; she frowns, sticks out her tongue, then mouths the word *retard* at him as he stumbles off the stand. Retard. He can read her lips. He glances the length of the row to his father, the murderer. His father tries to grin at him. Toby can detect the effort, the way the quivery ends of his father's fleshy lips twist down then up then down again. Suddenly Toby sneezes. Bringing the back of his wrist to his nose, making contact just in time with the stiff shirt cuff where it pokes out from the sweater's yellow sleeve, he lopes away with the cuff held to his face.

Nine

❖

For the first weeks, she could not recognize the season: stepping outside, she was always surprised to find the weather as it was, to find the weather at all. She no longer trusted the seasons. She no longer trusted air, sunlight, blue sky, or opening her eyes in the morning. The world was nothing you could trust anymore.

OFF THE ELEVATOR, before I even got near the windows at the end of the hall, sirens were wailing, several of them in different registers and tones, their discords layered on top of one another. In another section of the angry orchestra, car horns sounded, strident and insistent. I had just walked from my office along the bottlenecked streets, where only two or three vehicles were lucky to make it through any green light before it changed back to red. The pounding in my head from the noise became the percussion section. But Ibrahim's mother had already begun taking in stride these stymied emergencies, the frantic sights and sounds, and did not seem to notice the noise as she chattered with unusual ardor to an older woman I had never seen before. This woman was broader and taller, dressed in a drab, colorless robe-like affair, her face partly hidden by a headscarf but clearly beaming with smiles. Beside her stood a younger, shorter man with sparkling eyes in a clean, well-pressed mechanic's jumpsuit. The name AHMED was neatly embroidered in light blue thread over his chest pocket. He shifted his weight impatiently from one foot to the other, but smiled. It seemed the two of them were about to leave, but not able to say good-bye.

"This is Fatima, an old friend of Halima's, and her son-in-law Ahmed," Safiya explained to me. "Fatima and Halima were children together in Sudan. They lived in the same part of town, they played there, they got married there, their first babies played together, too."

The two old women laughed like schoolgirls, clasping each other's hands. "Like sisters," said Fatima, who spoke some English.

Safiya continued. "But Fatima and her husband, *Rahimahu Allah*, moved to Egypt and Halima hadn't seen her for more than twenty years, until now, these past weeks. Ahmed owns a car repair business in Weymouth. He has brought almost all his wife's family to America, one by one." She paused, playing with the end of her gauze headscarf before tossing it across her neck. I awaited this next installment of the Arabian nights, the story that would keep Ibrahim safe another day.

Safiya said, "We have just arranged for Ahmed to sell Ibrahim's car."

My heart thumped heavily. "Your car? The one you drive? You're selling it?"

"The one my brother has been driving," she corrected. "We do not need it anymore."

I bit my lip.

"So I will deposit the check for you," said Ahmed, shaking hands with Safiya. "It is a very good car and should sell quickly, for your asking price, *insh'Allah*."

The two older women locked together in a hug.

Safiya frowned, mirroring the expression on my face. "You know that it is time, Erika. We are set for next Thursday. You are happy for us, I know, that one of the nurses from this floor will come with us, Patricia, she is often here in the evenings. Yes? You remember? Tall and thin and always teasing him? She is very nice, and also she knows how to make Ibrahim obey. So it is all arranged now. For Patricia it is an adventure to go to Abu Dhabi, even to spend just a day or two. For us it is great to have someone who already knows what Ibrahim will need, someone he likes."

Safiya's brother Mahmoud said, "A nurse. A hospital bed. The intravenous set-up. A whole section of the plane, curtained off with—how many of us now?—eight, I think. That is how we are traveling."

"The sheikh is very generous," said Safiya.

"He better be," I said.

The two older friends let go of each other, weeping silently, and Ahmed escorted his mother-in-law down the hall.

Ten

❖

*Like the red-hot beams they found under the site weeks later; like the
remains they discovered here or there, at intervals further and further
apart, to be draped in a flag for a final farewell; like the caverns of
devastation and preservation that remained to be found down there:
that's what she had under her own tenuous hold on things, too. Her
own ground zero.*

THESE NEW KITCHENS mystify me. If you have enough money, you
slice carrots or assemble peanut butter and jelly sandwiches on a
granite countertop, like the surface of a tombstone before it is en-
graved. You are constantly reflected back to yourself in the stark
sheen of all stainless steel appliances, like fixtures in a morgue.
With all the work needed to keep them in high polish, who would
have time to cook? And how could anyone meet the expectations
of a professional chef's stove with its infinitely adjustable burn-
ers, its state-of-the-art ovens, its stainless facade frowning at you,
reproaching you, like a haughty, hairless purebred cat who never
budges from the kitchen but is always insulted by whatever you
put in its bowl. Only people who never cook could possibly want
these kitchens. But Nussbaum's wife cooks. Or seems to cook. As
the party gets started, she is in a kitchen like that, appearing to be
cooking, with a few genuine beads of perspiration on her flushed

forehead. Michael and Pammy Nussbaum have spent a fortune to *make* the kitchen like that, after gutting the perfectly good kitchen that was there before.

The disposable kitchen is a perk of democracy. The newer, better, and more desirable kitchen that looks like death is one of the rewards of grant after grant from the NIH, CDC, USAID. How fortunate Americans are, to have so generous an alphabet. We are waging wars without end so people like this have the right to have kitchens like that. From studying households in Africa that get poorer and poorer, a household in America can get richer and richer.

Lady Nussbaum continues to stir a gleaming copper-bottomed pot as she greets us. Thin, gamine, pixie-haired, she wears a sleek little black dress and spike-heeled shoes. Mother of three, she looks like her own daughter playing grown-up, but while her daughter would no doubt use make-up in her play, Lady N is radiantly au naturel—well-moisturized, and as unpainted as a freshly milled two-by-four. And petite. At least Nussbaum is actually taller than *someone*.

I should be incentivized by the glow of prosperity and opportunity that warms this house, but I am not. I should at least be jealous, but I am not. But I *am* uncomfortable. I am embarrassed by my little bowl of barley and vegetable salad, by Fiona's salsa and chips, by Ivan's quaint bottle of Georgian mountain *vin ordinaire*. Our potluck offerings are dwarfed, like we are dwarfed, us three graying outliers who arrived together on time, before anyone else, wearing jeans—whoops! We did not know it was a little-black-dress affair this holiday season—and we are dwarfed by the abundance and hugeness of roasts and casseroles and artisan breads that emerge from the Nussbaum ovens, by the unusual vintages brought upstairs at just the right temperature from the Nussbaum cellars, by the delicious meaty aromas (tinged with the fine hardwood cherry logs sizzling smokeless in the ornately-mantled fireplace) that permeate the many, many rooms of the Nussbaum manse.

This event does not feel so much like a potluck as the harvest-time reckoning of us ho-hum sharecroppers. In our involuntary tribute to noblesse oblige, we bring our meager offerings to the Lord of the Manor, so that he may experience his own plenty, his own power, his own delusion of beneficence all the more. So that we may revel, but also cower, in his presence, at his command. So that he may feel satisfied with his own good works, oblivious to our chafing or disintegration or disgust. Or maybe he is not oblivious but privately celebrates our various implosions.

"Help yourselves to drinks," says Nussbaum in a chummy tone as he carefully sets down two more bottles of Bordeaux among the array of liquor and fine microbrews, right beside Ivan's Kakheti, a bottle as simple and out of place among gentry as we are ourselves. I feel my back stiffen.

"It's okay," whispers Ivan, nudging me in the ribs with his elbow. "*Relax.*"

"But the terrorists are winning," I say.

"Nonsense."

It takes no time at all for the three of us to down the bottle of sturdy Georgian, which reinforces our peasant dispositions; but then, as others arrive, I move on to the vintage.

"Hello Sam! Hello Marcia! Hi Toby and Tina! Hi Clare! Hi Winnie and Brad! Welcome, everyone!" Nussbaum greets folks at the door with the same unsagging grin all evening. The overhead lighting at the doorway bestows on his hair a golden sheen.

"Please make yourselves at home," Lady Nussbaum calls out from the kitchen, which opens into the dining area, which opens into the first cavernous living room, which opens into the second. She wipes her forehead with the back of the hand clutching a preposterously long carving knife. An immense baked turkey roosts on the countertop.

Finally a large contingent of other colleagues has arrived. A world music CD is turned up, talk and laughter get noisier, and my colleagues and their kin are milling around, pouring drinks, plunging chips into guacamole, slicing paté, smearing baba ganoosh onto pitas. We are no longer lonely sharecroppers. It feels suddenly like a party.

I wander from room to room, glass of fine Bordeaux in hand.

"You haven't heard?" asks Toby. Loudly, he begins to hold forth on the fucked-up Nairobi study to Sue and Winnie and Clare, assistants for other projects and lowly occupants of the harem whose departure dates are so far undeclared but inevitable nonetheless. I try to involve myself in another conversation, but every so often Toby's voice booms through.

"So what does she do? She feels sorry for them. She *gives* them stuff!" he booms. It annoys me, the mileage he tries to get from this story.

"And Frances is like totally bouncing off the walls." He laughs very loudly now. The women of the harem laugh with him. It is easy to laugh at Frances, so set in her habits and so far away. Toby mimics Frances in a high-pitched voice, a voice Frances doesn't even have. "Now the household data is all con*tam*inated. It's dis*tor*ted. What are we gonna do-oooh-ooh?"

He allows a little time for the harem women to laugh again. And they do. They shriek with laughter, while he beams and grins and makes fun of the woman who somehow slipped ahead.

"So I figure, once we get an estimate of how much it came to, we can count it like they went out and made some pocket change. Really, how much could it actually be? It couldn't be very much. Bertha couldn't have *had* very much. We didn't *pay* her very much."

Winnie says, "Maybe she stole it. Maybe she embezzled."

"Naaah. The books are clean. I checked. No, whatever it was, it's a drop in the bucket. Like one of the kids in a household went out and got a job mowing lawns or babysitting or something. We just enter it into the 'miscellaneous income' column for the last couple of months. I can handle that."

Mowing lawns in the slums of the Third World. Babysitting for pocket money. He's completely clueless. But that doesn't stop him.

Pammy sets the huge platter of turkey on the buffet table behind Toby. "Can somebody help me carve the leg of lamb? Please?" She waves the ridiculous carving knife in the air again. Everyone shrugs, looks around. "No carvers in this department?"

I say, "Toby, how about you?" My voice bypasses my brain. It didn't used to do that.

"Me?"

"Yeah, isn't it sort of in your heritage?"

"Huh?"

"Didn't you once say your father was a butcher?"

Toby's pasty face turns deep scarlet. "No I did *not*. I *never* said anything like that."

"His father was a teacher," says Tina, his wife, rapidly patting Toby's shoulder with one hand while balancing the baby in her other arm. "A high school science teacher."

"Oh, sorry," I say. "I must have confused you with somebody else."

Tina says, "It sure smells good in here. Meat and bread and apples and cinnamon and wood and everything."

I say, "But then, if he was a biology guy, he would be good at dissection, your dad, wouldn't he?"

"And I *love* this old mantelpiece," says Tina. "Where did it come from?"

"Believe it or not, it was once a headboard for a very fancy bed," says Lord Nussbaum, who has finally taken charge of the carving board. "From France. Nineteenth-century France."

"Eighteenth-century," Pammy calls out from the far end of the buffet table, which is now almost fully laden with food. She is seeing to finishing touches: serving spoons, hot pads, spoon rests, several matching pewter candlesticks placed just so.

"Dissection is like an academic form of butchery," I say.

"We used to dissect frogs in school," adds Fiona, with a bit of a *frisson*. "You couldn't pass biology without cutting up the damn frog."

"It's such a quaint word, *butchery*," adds Ivan. "You see butcheries on the streets of Uganda and Kenya. That's what they call a meat market there, from the British influence, I guess. A butchery."

"Damnit!" shouts Toby. He flings a plastic spoon in my direction, but it is too lightweight to make the full arc and falls harmlessly to the floor. He glares straight at me, purple in the face. The room falls silent, holding its collective breath in the aftershocks of Toby's odd show of temper. He seems to be just barely containing a rage far bigger than this one brief outburst. Maybe it is hereditary after all.

Tina moves beside me and speaks in a soft voice—not a whisper, not a secret or confidential voice—seemingly her words are addressed to me but I think they are also meant for everyone to overhear. "Toby's dad died when he was just a little kid. He barely knew him. That's why he's so sensitive. That's why he doesn't like to talk about him."

She sounds perfectly sincere. She has the misty, trusting eyes of someone who believes what she is saying. I realize that even Tina may not know the truth.

"I'm so sorry," I say. "I was only being silly. I was only cutting up." I look straight at Toby. He winces. "I'm so sorry."

"I'm so sorry, too," says Ivan. Though God knows why.

"Yeah," mumbles Toby, still glaring at me, at me alone. "Okay."

Now at least he is subdued for the rest of the evening. No more flaunting someone else's failure for his own sake.

IN THE CAR, after the party, after the car's heat has roared on and we have dropped Fiona off, Ivan pulls over to the curb and turns to me. "Why were you being so nasty to Toby?"

"I can't tell you."

"Why can't you tell me?"

"I can't tell you why I can't tell you. I can't tell you anything. I've sworn not to."

"Sworn to Toby?" he asks, his face scrunched in an earnest attempt at understanding.

"In a way, yeah." I crack open my window to keep from suffocating.

"What do you mean, 'in a way'?"

"He doesn't know it. That I've sworn not to tell."

"Then you haven't sworn to Toby. If he never asked you to."

I sigh a long sigh. "He can't. He couldn't have. I can't tell him. He doesn't know."

"Doesn't know what?"

"That's what I'm talking about. I can't tell *you* what I can't tell *him*. Just trust me please, it's for his sake."

Exasperated, Ivan drums his fingers on the steering wheel. "It's just so unlike you, to be so mean."

"These days, *everything* is like me. Nothing is unlike me."

"I don't understand what 'these days' are."

I feel a lump in my throat. "And I thought you were the one person who did."

Ivan sighs. "The attacks? Your grief? I don't see why that would make you mean to Toby. Especially when you go out of your way to be kind to other people. Your students, for example."

I roll my window down another inch. "He gets off on his own ignorance. He builds himself up on the backs of project people in another country he doesn't know the first thing about."

118

"He's inexperienced. He's learning."

"But he's not in school. This isn't on-the-job training, it's his work in the real world. What he does so blithely and in such ignorance has consequences."

"C'mon, he's just a project manager."

"He's Nussbaum's little pet. Nussbaum feeds him scraps of his own ego."

"That's not an excuse for meanness. Gratuitous, unprovoked— my God, public!" Ivan clutches his forehead with one hand.

"It's an explanation, not an excuse. Anyway nobody even noticed. And it only seems gratuitous because you don't know what I know."

He pounds the steering wheel. "But I have no *clue* what you're talking about."

I'm exasperated, too. "Right. That's the idea. I can't tell you. You can't know. I've sworn I can't tell."

"But sworn to whom? If not to Toby?"

I sit quietly for a minute. Ivan looks expectant.

"To-by or not To-by, that is the question." I laugh. My laughter, unaccompanied, sounds tinny and dissolves out the window. "What a screech I am."

Ivan sighs, frowning. "No you're not. That's not even funny. Not *now*."

I am quiet for another minute. It's freezing. I roll my window back up.

"I'm sorry," I say finally.

"Are you really sorry?"

"About what?"

119

He grits his teeth. "Why are you being so difficult? About being nasty to Toby."

"That? No. Not really. The distinctions are important, that's why I'm being so difficult. I'm not sorry about being nasty to Toby. But I'm sorry I can't tell you."

"Tell me what?"

"Anything about it at all."

He puts the car into gear and drives me back to his place for the night.

Eleven

❖

She felt as if she was already a ghost, a vestige of something she didn't understand, never understood. As if life had somehow already ended, and she was still accidentally here.

I KNOW THIS about Faith, the orphan girl: she is twelve years old. She is not a research subject or a cohort population or a household number; she's not a project or participant or demographic. She's a girl. Flesh and blood. Exactly five feet, one-and-a-half inches tall, she can sprint like an Olympic medalist and do five-digit sums in her head. But her father died first, and then, only three years later, her mother. From AIDS of course. Now she lives in her aunt's corrugated-iron-roofed shack in the Kibera slum, a shack so small that all the children must sleep together: she and her little brother and her four cousins, two boys and two girls. Timothy, her fifteen-year-old cousin, a silent skinny kid, the oldest, can get to her at night. He sticks his finger in. Then he rubs himself. He can get to her when she goes the short way for water, too. His hands go underneath her skirt. He pushes her roughly to the ground. He doesn't care who's around, he barely pulls her out of sight. Here in the city people are used to pretending not to see. She tries to take the long way to the spigot, a path too crowded for his monkey-business, but a full plastic jerrican is much too heavy on her head for that much time. Once, carrying it back home through the shortcut, she saw him and flung the water at him, then ran. But she had to go back for water again and wait again in the long, snaky line.

She has spunk; you can certainly say that about her. She goes to school and used to be good in her lessons, but has been falling a little further behind every day, every week. That's hardly a surprise, with all the chores. Not just the water fetching, the wood-scrap hunting, the sweeping, the pot scrubbing, the clothes washing at the spigot far away; she has to do most of the cooking, too, when there is anything to cook. But she is only allowed to eat what's left after the others have helped themselves. Often nothing is left. So secretly she feeds on the tiniest of bits of food while she's cooking, scrapings of half-raw potatoes or hard kernels of maize, she has to suck on them, not chewing, not moving her mouth, or her aunt will see. Sometimes her aunt notices anyway or guesses and beats her with a shoe.

"Dirty little thief! What would your mother say if she was alive?"

"I wouldn't be here if she was alive," says the girl simply, without petulance. "I wouldn't be *here*, and I wouldn't be *hungry*."

Her aunt clobbers her on the shoulders with the shoe, then backs off. "You think *she* would have had more food on the table? You think *she'd* do better? The one who couldn't even figure out how to *stay alive*!" She throws the shoe at her niece, then turns away and cries.

The girl still attends school; however listless and hungry and unprepared and tired and beaten she may sometimes be, she gets herself there against almost all odds. She loves arithmetic, she loves English, she loves science. But love of her studies, pluck, spunk, God, and determination can take her just so far. Sometimes now she misses days when she has her bleeding because there is no place decent and private for girls to go and the rags she uses are impossible. Yes, rags. It is the twenty-first century and menstrual blood in this world of ours still flows on rags. If she can't change them, if she can't wash them, they leak onto the bench, they smell. She can hold in her urine all day, but not her blood. The absence of a sink and the foul latrine finally triumphs over what had seemed to be her endless pluck, her endless spunk. She tries to study at home those days. But if she is home on a school day when that other woman comes, the one who asks the questions, her aunt makes her hide. If she is home on a day when her aunt has a man, she hides herself. But where? One of the men has touched her. He looks for her, he finds her crouching outside, he laughs a loud laugh. This time he laughs. This time he goes away.

I KNOW THIS about the researcher from the United States: Frances lives in Karen, just a few miles outside Nairobi, in a bungalow in a gated compound. To get home, she has to pass through two different checkpoints guarded by very tall, very black unsmiling *askaris* with rifles. Her bungalow is surrounded by a wall, and when she honks the horn of the Land Cruiser her kitchen girl has to unlock and open the doors so she can drive through. Likewise, the girl has to open and then quickly lock up the doors in the wall as soon as Frances drives away in the morning. The girl hums all the time. She hums hymns. Frances doesn't like them, but she doesn't say anything, she permits the noise simply to grate on her, like a buzzing fly that comes and goes. The girl spends all of her Sundays, her one day off, at church; she believes fervently that she has been saved. Frances believes nothing. No, that's not true. She rejects the theory of God, but she believes in human progress on both the individual and collective level and she has organized her life around that belief.

Frances eats oatmeal for breakfast just about every morning, and every evening she brushes her long, brown hair with one hundred strokes after unpinning it from its workaday knot. She collects cactus plants. She has a little garden where she coaxes Swiss chard and arugula and little Japanese eggplants out of the red soil, in addition to the usual greens and tomatoes and yams already familiar to the girl. Sometimes they work side by side in the garden, and the girl hums then, too. Frances has a mango tree and a banana tree. The weather is good here; it's no wonder the British settlers were drawn to these hills, their lovely breezes and cool nights with no humidity. But she still suffers from anxiety and takes pills. She always did, even as a teenager in Evanston, but it got worse at Antioch and later in graduate school; this anxiety did not start in Kenya. Neither does it end here. She can't tolerate anyone standing behind her. If she's in a public place, she almost never sits down; she always has to keep maneuvering so no one is behind her back.

She doesn't really have friends here in Nairobi, she never even talks to the other white people who are her uphill neighbors in this part of Karen. Once in a while she goes out for dinner with Christine Mwangi, a colleague from the university who is listed in the grant as a local partner; there is one table at the Holiday Inn restaurant where Frances can sit with her back to the wall, virtu-ally against the wall. No one can get behind her there, not even a waiter. She never goes to the buffet or salad bar because someone is always behind you when you stand in line. She never stands in lines. If she has to meet with people outside her office, the Holiday Inn is always where she goes, and this is the table where she always sits. This is where she meets Christine and puts both dinners on her expense account.

Not too far from the bungalow in Karen there is also a café in a shopping center where she can get a good brunch and a seat against the wall. In fact in a corner. The best. A good Sunday morn-ing outing for Frances, about once a month, is pancakes and strong coffee and the British papers with her back against the wall at the corner table. There is no joy in her life, but she doesn't expect any, she doesn't even want any. Not that she is unhappy, but joy is an idea she abandoned long ago. It just didn't apply. Pancakes suffice. Work suffices. It is hard to imagine what she is always working at, but she is always working. At the office she doesn't leave her desk all day, and she often sits at her desk at home working late into the evening. Even on her exercise bike, which she pedals exactly thirty-five minutes every single day, increasing the resistance to make the ride harder and harder as she goes along, she is reading. Her reports back to the office in Boston are voluminous. Nobody will ever fault her for lack of detail. The project is moving along very well.

I KNOW THIS about Bertha, the project assistant: she has a university degree on her CV but has studied for only two-and-a-half years and has not gone back to finish. Not yet. Sometimes she has four households to visit in one day, and she's angry at Frances because it means she can't spend enough time in any one of them. There is no earthly reason why they have to be bunched up like that. Frances just says so. They could be staggered so that the questions she must ask every month, the same questions, every month, fall twenty-eight or thirty days from the previous visit. She could keep track of that easily. She's no dummy. All the visits do not have to be in the first week of the month. The growth monitoring she does on children every three months could be spaced differently, too. But Frances never asks her opinion, and most days Bertha is stuck in the office, bound in by stupid rules for no good reason. And there's no intervention—that's what *they* call what *she* calls *help*; nothing is planned or budgeted until after the study's fourth year. Everybody could be dead by then.

She tries not to be bitter. It would take so little to help these families. She sees the need in each of the households, yet she is not allowed to give them anything. But actually she does. She has found a way to give. She takes office supplies, she knows it is really stealing but it is better to steal from the shameful waste of the Americans than to let people starve, she is certain of that, she has to order so much stuff anyway, the way Frances goes through it all, what waste! Nobody notices—Frances doesn't notice, and there is nobody else to notice or not notice. What she takes is a drop in the bucket, the budget is so huge. So she orders more than they could ever possibly use, little by little she pilfers it and orders more, each month she makes a bigger order, but still it has never been so big that Frances notices. Then she gets Charles, a guy she knows from her same hometown, to sell the stuff. It's easy for him, he makes a good living selling stolen merchandise: cameras, guns, agricultural equipment, electrical generators, toilets, ID cards. For Charles, they are also a mere drop in the bucket, her boxes of pens and Post-it notes and ink cartridges and copier toner and scissors and files. He takes none of the proceeds from her sales, they are too pitiful, he is too honorable in his own way; he gives her cash and then she buys food and school uniforms for the families with some of the money and gives some of the money as cash outright. Ink cartridges and copier toner do best. Post-it notes are big. Pens and paper and tape are hardly worth the effort.

I KNOW THIS about Mary, the head of the household now: when the study started, Muthai was head of the household, because a man always says he is head of the household whether or not he does anything at all to head it, and Muthai only did anything at all at rare and random moments, even in the best of times, if any times could be said to have been the best of times, probably not. Even when he first brought them to the city and worked as a tout for the *matatus* and had at least a little money all the time, that period could not be called even good times, let alone best of times. But he hasn't been around for months now. Mary has lost track how many. He shouted about all the kids, he swore at her sister's kids, he took a swat at Timothy, his own oldest boy, who dodged it, and then he walked away without another word. Like he was just going out for a drink. She believed he'd gone around the corner to his regular hole-in-the-wall bar. Maybe for a while he was there that night. But she hasn't seen him since. The guy at the bar said Muthai was never there at all, but she knows the guy at the bar lies all the time. At first she would wonder: did Muthai leave her and move in with another woman? Was he run over by a car or murdered by scoundrels? Was he wasting away from sickness or dead already? She has not found a way to find out. Something in her doesn't care enough to make the effort. And the children don't even ask about him anymore. He wasn't supposed to be sick but maybe he was. He was always thin, but he didn't seem any thinner the last time she saw him. She doesn't know if anyone will even tell her if he dies. Only if one of his brothers wants to have her, but probably not, not with this crowd of kids. Most days she sits coughing a lot on the bare ground in front of the shack, in the hour or two or three before the sun goes down, peeling back the husks from a few ears of corn, coughing, setting the ears to roast on the makeshift charcoal grill. Sometimes she can sell five or six ears in a day. Sometimes she can get yams to roast and sell pieces of those, too. She and a few other women scratch some edibles out of a tiny rectangle of nearly barren soil over by the railroad track. One of the others also trades at the market and brings back the odd item to sell. And then there are the men who will pay her a few shillings for sex, when she needs to buy charcoal or food. And Bertha sometimes brings money from the research study. The payments do not come at regular times or in regular amounts, but they eventually come. When Bertha brings money, Mary does not have to go to the bar in search of men for a few days. And that is about as good as it gets for poor Mary.

Twelve

❖

*Not fifty thousand. Not one hundred thousand. It was only three
thousand some. And then, it turned out, even fewer. But so what? Did
that make any difference?*

FOUR DAYS HAD passed since my last visit; I felt remiss. They were
standing huddled around a weeping Safiya in the encampment by
the window, frowning at me as I came down the hall past Ibrahim's
closed door: Ibrahim's parents, Hassan, the academic couple from
Rhode Island, Gabriel's daughters. Ibrahim's sister Saleha, sitting in
the corner, looked morosely at her embroidery, her hands motionless on her lap. My heart thumped hard; something terrible must
have happened with Ibrahim. So this was it, this is how it would
end. I held my breath as I got closer. They stared at me and did not
open their circle to let me in.

"The police have taken Mahmoud, Safiya's brother," said
Gabriel's daughter, the engineer, turning from the circle to face me.

"Ibrahim is okay?" I was light-headed with relief for a second
or two—it was not Ibrahim, Ibrahim was okay! But then a deeper
dread kicked in.

"Ibrahim is the same," said Safiya, also turning toward me.
Her face seemed even more haggard, more distressed than during

all these weeks of her husband's slow demise. "But Mahmoud is suddenly a terrorist."

"What?"

"He was driving me Tuesday to Whole Foods in Ibrahim's car. We were only a few blocks from the apartment. The inspection sticker had expired but we never noticed."

"With everything going on, how would you notice?" said Hassan, who began pacing in a tight circle of his own.

"A state trooper stopped him for the sticker. And then we didn't have the registration; I had left it in a bag at home. Stupid me!" Her voice caught. "I explained, and they seemed to believe me, but they spent a long time looking at Mahmoud's Sudanese passport, they said things about his Saudi visa and work permit, they made calls on their phone." For a long moment she held her headscarf over her face to hide her tears. Then she composed herself. "*My* passport with my residence permit in the UAE and my tourist visa here they accepted. They told me to go home, with my two violation tickets and my two big fines, but they told Mahmoud to get out of the car. He was angry, and when he is angry he stops talking. They did not like his silence. They put handcuffs on him and shoved him hard into the back of the police car." Her voice broke again.

Hassan took over. "Now we don't even know where he is. It is two days, and the lawyer we got is still trying to find out where he is. The consulate is working on it, even the Senator's office."

"Detained! Like he's a terrorist!" cried the tall Professor Hamid.

"Disappeared," murmured the petite Professor Hamid. "Like in a bad dream. Like the worst nightmare."

"Like a police state," I blurted.

"We did not think this would happen here," said Hassan.

"It should *not* happen here," I said.

"We should have known better," said Gabriel's daughter, the anthropologist.

"He'll be okay," chirped her sister. "You are all so negative. It's just a mistake. This is Boston, not Khartoum for heaven's sake. He will be out in no time."

Everyone smiled indulgently at her as if she were a deluded small child.

"We are not telling Ibrahim," warned Safiya, turning back to me. "He must never know. He must not worry."

"But you! Now *you* have this worry!" Finally I got close enough to hug her. She held me tight.

"I am so sorry," I said to her. "I am so sorry," I said to everyone.

Hassan translated for Ibrahim's parents. They replied in Arabic. "They say thank you, but it is not your fault."

"WE DO NOT say good-byes tonight," Safiya said to me. "Tomorrow you'll come before we leave. The flight will be quite late at night. We will be many, plus the nurse and equipment. Mahmoud had to go back early, you know." She flashed a quick, false smile, then, turning so Ibrahim couldn't see, let an exhausted grimace deflate her face. "He had to get back to his job. So without his help, we will have to give ourselves more time. We will leave here by five with the ambulance, the taxis, the van with the luggage, everything. Come at four o'clock and we will say our farewells then."

Lying very flat in the bed, Ibrahim took my hand and smiled. "So save your beautiful words for tomorrow, okay?"

"So now I should not say, You taught me so much, Ibrahim. *You* have been *my* teacher all along." Already I fought a lump in my throat.

He laughed. "No. Don't say it now. I won't say either how much I thank you. For your friendship. Your freewriting. Your sacks of potatoes and bridges and riverbanks. Your pathetic Judaism. The oranges."

"Tomorrow!" interjected Hassan.

I let go of his hand and backed slowly toward the door.

His face became very serious. "Thank you," he said.

"See you tomorrow," I said.

"See you tomorrow," he said.

"Thank you," I said.

"Tomorrow!" shouted Safiya, laughing, grabbing my shoulders. Then in a low voice: "It will be hard enough tomorrow, so let's not make ourselves sad today, too." She hugged me and kissed both my cheeks. Ibrahim's mother hugged me and kissed my cheeks, wordless but smiling. Saleha hugged me and said many things in Arabic I could not understand, wiping her cheeks. I grabbed the hand Ibrahim's father offered and shook it wildly.

"See you tomorrow at four," I said. I took a glance at the encampment, which had shrunk to just a few chairs, Saleha's embroidery, and a single prayer rug.

But when I got there at four o'clock the next afternoon, the room was empty. Not only had the encampment at the end of the hallway disappeared, there were no people, no things in the room.

The bed was stripped bare. Only one empty chair occupied the corner. All was silent. It was as if they had never been there at all.

"He left before noon," said a nurse. "Everyone with him. The plane was at four."

Thirteen

❖

She is in a small plane high in the sky with Ivan in the pilot's seat. She didn't know he could pilot a plane. They are somewhere near Albany, heading south, flying over the Hudson River, down its length; she sees the river, she sees bridges spanning it at Rhinecliff, Poughkeepsie, the Tappan Zee. Soon the George Washington Bridge will be visible, too. But she didn't think they were going to New York; they were supposed to be going west. And something is wrong below: black clouds of smoke billow up. She wonders if there's just been a crash—or an explosion? A bomb? She has the sudden nightmare certainty that it is happening again, the attack on New York, and their little plane is right in the middle. Her panic begins. Ivan points down: she can see the city from here, the skyscrapers, the rivers east and west, the ocean harbor, the stunningly straight lines of the big avenues, Central Park a near-perfect rectangle. But to their right, where he is pointing, is the rim of fire. New Jersey is engulfed by flames. The line of burning devastation is advancing across the landscape. She knows that nothing will escape it, and yet Ivan begins to bring them down. No, she yells. Not yet! Go farther! They could still escape. But she feels the descent; he is aiming to land. He says nothing. She glares at him. But now it is not Ivan piloting the plane, it is Toby. He grins. And she becomes frantic, trembling and ready to scream even after she awakes. Or maybe she has already screamed.

What's wrong? Ivan sits up.

She reaches over and touches him, in bed beside her.

ONE EARLY WEDNESDAY evening Bertha makes an unofficial visit to Kibera. She finds the orphan girl crouched in the little patch of dust outside in back of the shack, scrubbing the burned bottom of a pot. Bertha sees a small basin of dirty water on the ground. She spots Timothy, the cousin, and the way he eyes the girl as he slouches against the shack wall. The girl avoids his leer, avoids him. Something's not right.

When the boy slinks out of sight, she hands Faith a bag with a box of sanitary pads inside. "If you use these, you will be able to go to school when you're bleeding."

The girl says nothing. She takes the bag with her left hand, the hand that is not so wet or chafed with scrubbing but still sends muddy rivulets running down the arm. She is barely covered by two worn-out cloths tied around her.

"I'll bring more next time," says Bertha.

And six weeks later Bertha brings another plastic bag with another box inside and the girl is alone and scrubbing what seems to be the same battered pot in the same circle of dirt, which after a sudden cloudburst is now soft mud. Bertha hands her the bag. The girl frees one wet hand from the pot, but then she drops the handle of the bag. The box falls out of the bag onto the ground, the pale pink wrapping and the plain drawing and the printed words of sanitary pads now right out in the open, spilled on the dirt, canceling out any secret of her monthly blood. Nobody else is there to see, but still Faith bursts into tears; she hides her face behind both hands, one hand still clutching the soapy bit of rag. Are these tears from embarrassment or shame? wonders Bertha. Or something else? The girl weeps; for a few unbearable minutes she refuses to uncover her face or say anything to Bertha. But at last she picks up the box, puts it in the bag, and goes into the shack; Bertha follows her. Bertha sees the corner where the girl keeps her few things, the blouse and skirt for school hanging limply on a wooden peg. The girl stuffs the bag into the corner. Next to it is a bag with a box inside. A bag with the same unopened box of sanitary pads that Bertha brought last time, six weeks ago.

Now Bertha sees that the skinny boy skulks around again outside.

How can she stop what is happening?

In the doorway of Frances's office, Bertha blurts it out: "I think one of the Kibera orphans is pregnant. Household number nine."

Frances rolls her eyes. "Like it's never happened before." She looks back down at her desk.

"But this is very bad."

"Isn't it always very bad?" Frances's eyes stay on her papers.

"I think it's the older cousin in the household, the aunt's son, who abuses her. Nobody stops him. They all sleep in the same room. I think her cousin made her pregnant. She is only twelve. She only just started menstruating a few months ago and now she stopped."

"Did she tell you the cousin raped her?"

"No of course not. She would not dare."

Frances looks up at Bertha. "So maybe he didn't."

"I'm sure she's pregnant."

"Maybe she has been with other boys, not her cousin. Maybe she has even been with older men."

Bertha looks down at her feet. "She is very young and very scared."

"Or maybe it's malnutrition that stopped her period."

Bertha looks back at Frances. "There could also be malnutrition. She is extremely thin. They all take from the pot before she is allowed, I think. But also the biggest boy cousin has a look."

"A look?"

"You know what I mean, I think. Like a bird of prey."

Frances sighs a very big sigh, standing up from her desk.

"Like the girl is a mouse, with no hope of escaping the vulture's eye," says Bertha.

Frances sighs again. "You think this is our problem? We are flies on the wall, observing what would happen anyway, whether we were there or not." She stands now, as she often does, with her back firmly against the wall. Like she *is* a fly on the wall, thinks Bertha.

"But we are not observing *thisss*." Bertha lets the end of the word prolong in a hiss. "And if we are there like flies but are not watching *thissss*, we are letting it happen."

Frances stares at her for a long moment. "You think we're aiding and abetting? You think we're accomplices?"

"I did not say that we are *making it happen*." She did not say it, but that is what she fears the most: that they are making it happen. "But we are not *stopping* what is in front of our eyes."

"You don't understand observational research," says Frances.

Bertha lowers her eyes again, silent, while Frances stares straight at her.

"You don't understand the way studies are designed and how they must be carried out, *by the book*, to be accurate and objective," says Frances.

138

Bertha looks up again. "I understand what is happening in front of our eyes."

Frances laughs. "The whole damn fucked-up *country* is in front of our eyes! Am I responsible for all—" Frances stops. Bertha has flinched, as if slapped hard in the face. Frances sighs another big sigh. "Enough. I'll look into it." Frances waves Bertha away, like a fly.

But Frances is, after all (and Frances would say above all) a woman of conscience; she decides to see for herself. She borrows a driver from another project and he takes her deep into Kibera, where she has never set foot before. And it is amazing what she does not see, even when she is finally there. She does not see the mounds of tomatoes and greens and mangos and beans at the bustling marketplace beside the tracks. She does not see the hungry, idle boys, shirtless and shoeless, stalking the narrowest alleyways like feral dogs; nor does she see other children, also shoeless but in very white threadbare shirts, singing their hearts out in a makeshift open-air church. She does not see three men carrying an intricately carved mahogany table along the alley toward a neatly bricked shack or the four matching mahogany straight chairs, still perched on the edge of a pickup truck. She does not see the nineteen women with jerricans standing silently in line at a water kiosk. No, Frances sees only her own feet and the exact spot where she puts each one of them, step after step. The driver walks directly in front of her as he leads her from the car and over the slimy stream of muck to a solid dirt path. Then up an embankment, across the railroad tracks, down again. Too late she realizes he has not thought out the route well, he has parked the car wrong, too far. As they race along, she now insists he follow right behind her, so at least no one else can. Finally she sees Mary husking corn, the shriveled uneven-teethed ears that were picked too soon roasting on a little brazier. This is when she begins to talk with Mary. This is when Mary says, "We are grateful for the payments."

Frances's back is almost pressed against the shack, but not quite, who knows what filth harbors there, what bacteria or fungus could be growing on it, what bugs and worms crawl; she leaves a deliberate but potentially dangerous inch between her back and this wall that isn't really a wall anyway, just wattled sticks and mud. It is with her back not-quite-against the not-really-a-wall that she finally learns that Bertha gives out money and school uniforms and food to this household. She surmises that Bertha likely gives to other project households, too, violating every rule, putting the whole orphan project in danger. Screwing up everything.

She does not even wonder where Bertha gets the money.

For a moment, a very long moment, a moment that Frances never finishes, the girl's pregnancy is forgotten, while Bertha's goose gets thrown into a pot on a high flame. It does not take long to cook a goose here, no longer than the path back to the car, up and down embankments, across tracks, over a reeking ditch of sewage. It does not take long for Frances to fire Bertha from what she should have remembered was an excellent job and the luckiest of breaks, this job, this excellent job, especially for someone like her, especially for someone like Bertha. But she blew it. Boy oh boy did she blow it. Before the short conversation is over, Frances reminds her again how lucky she was to have had this job, this plum.

Bertha hears the words: someone like you. Especially. For. The words echo everywhere even after Frances stops spitting them out like watermelon seeds, one by one. Lucky. Break. Especially. For. Someone. Like. You.

Her thoughts drift away from the hot stream of Frances's anger. What *is* someone like me, Bertha wonders. Who *am* I, to be someone like? Who are the others, who are like me? Would I recognize them if I saw them? A few days later, she takes the girl to the place she already knows, the private clinic where one doctor does abortions in secret. To pay for it she has sold all the last cartridges of copier toner to Charles at triple the usual price. She has had to pay her price, too, she has paid a tax, but at least Charles agreed to put on the condom. He is used to condoms, it turns out. Now *that* is what's lucky, really. That's how she is lucky, for someone like her: a man agrees to a condom. If he hadn't, well, she cannot think of what choice she would have made. It does not bear thinking. He is an old acquaintance, almost a friend. He is not rough. It doesn't really matter, this unfeeling coupling that she has with him on flattened cardboard boxes behind the electrical generators. It does not matter to her, though it seems to matter to *him*. Otherwise why include it in the price? For him, it must be added value. Afterward, cleaning herself with a paper towel stolen from the Americans, she wonders if maybe it never matters to *someone like her*. Whoever that is.

As the girl, crying, rises slowly from a bench when her name is called, Bertha squeezes her hand tightly, and walks with her to the cubicle.

Fourteen

❖

In a dream she realizes she is married. She has a husband whose voice she hears, but she does not see him and can't make out what he's saying; his voice becomes fainter and fainter as she is somehow uprooted from home, forced to flee. She has a daughter who she tries to protect. They wander, they crouch in bushes, hiding from fighters running past, hiding from explosions and gunshots. They are too cold. They are too hot. They suffer for what must be a long time. If she sleeps at all, she sleeps with her eyes open. There are no houses left, only rubble and brambles and brush. They are drenched in rain, then parched and sunburned. They are dirty; their hair grows long, uncombed. They forage for food. They stop talking to one another, there is nothing left to say. They are barefoot, their feet scraped and calloused and black with dirt. She is aware that they have become unrecognizable—but to whom? There is nobody anymore to see them, not even soldiers running past. She finally stumbles onto a road. A car appears, and she flags it down. It stops. Inside is a man whose look she doesn't like or trust: he is stocky, unsmiling, mustachioed, with a receding hairline. Who could he be? Which side is he on? Suddenly she knows he is that same man who was once her husband. He doesn't recognize her. He doesn't recognize her as his wife or even, she realizes, as a person, as a human. Because she is so far gone now. Because she no longer even feels fear now. He says, You must be the sister of my cat. Then: Sit in the back. But where is her daughter now? She opens the car's back door, but where is her daughter? She wakes herself and tries not to fall asleep again, afraid to find herself in the same dream.

THE DAY IS uncannily warm, clear, blue-skied, you would not look at this day through a dirt-streaked hotel window, as we did, or walk through a uniform-guarded set of doors out into the day as it begins on West 23rd Street, as we did, and say it is mid-winter. No, this is not what a mid-winter morning in New York would look or feel like. Even the wind, though persistent, is too nonchalant, the papers blowing around the gutter are too sprightly, the cashier at Murray's Bagels too uncomplaining, even the occasional fluffy cloud skittering across deep blue is too whimsical for winter, and yet it *is*. It is mid-January. It is *only* mid-January, four months since.

I do not want to get tickets for the Ground Zero viewing platform, I make it clear to Ivan that I do not want to go up to the platform at all, but when we get close, when we are stopped in our first numbness by posters and pictures of the missing and handwritten remembrances and deep layers of improvised heartbreak still clinging to the walls and fences, an overly solicitous policeman, steeped in the kindness of his broken band of brothers, urges us onto the line. "There's no need for tickets," he says, "when it's not crowded, like now. You got lucky."

I hold back anyway.

"Go on up." He gestures to the line.

My mouth opens, then closes without a word.

Ivan whispers, "It would be an insult to *him*, not to go." He takes my hand and pulls me along. "The man *wants* crowds. He *needs* us."

It is only eight o'clock. Lower Manhattan's semi-sobered buzz has not yet really begun for the day, just the clang of food vendors and news stands and trucks, the *whooshing*, squealing undercurrent of traffic, a few gasping buses, a distant jackhammer *rat-tat-tatting*. But as we start up the ramp, the pinstriped man in line in front of us jabbers bonds trading on his cell phone with stunning crassness. Is this not a sacred site? Are not infinitesimal remains of his own acquaintances and colleagues lost forever in this soil? For several moments he does not notice when the line moves forward; too engrossed in preventing a disastrous sale, he traps us yards and yards behind the line which snakes along farther away from him, away from us. In a case of such unspeakable disrespect, Ivan and I debate the etiquette of jumping the line: are we mourners or voyeurs? Voyeurs can jump, mourners can't, says Ivan. Isn't it the other way around? I ask. But finally the same, kind policeman taps Mr. Pinstripe on the shoulder. Phone at his ear, he strides ahead to catch up to the line, still trading. Why would he even come to Ground Zero? From what checklist must he cross off this pilgrimage?

"Wait," I say to Ivan. I lead him to the side of the ramp and let a Chinese family with several little children pass us. I let three sad-faced, middle-aged women in ski parkas pass us. A young, silent, and solemn blue-jeaned couple passes us, too, both in black pea-coats, holding hands. These people are my buffer from the trader.

"Okay." We step back in line, now in front of a cluster of German-speaking tourists who lag a bit. As we round the next stage of the ramp I hear occasional guttural German undertones in back, bursts of Chinese in front, but at least not the stabbing cell phone pitch.

Soon, too soon, we are standing exactly where we have been going. We are here, overlooking. The deep and deeper site, which stretches out in all directions. It is no longer heaped with rubble and debris; it is eerily emptied, except for an amalgamation of stilled machinery, giant cranes and earth-movers, occasional piles of who knows what, sinister puddles, and the irrefutable truth of scorched bedrock. It has been picked through, vacated bucket by bucket and truck by truck, parts bulldozed, the sides shored up with strangely quaint, low-tech wooden beams. It is both too vast and too small for me to comprehend. How could so many square blocks of city vanish? And yet how did those mammoth towers ever fit within the confines of these fences?

I look up: I once went somewhere in that airy void for a meeting with a state agency. I look down: under here somewhere I scurried from job to job with thousands of others; I ate frozen chocolate yogurt. In a discount store that no longer exists I bought shoes that gave me blisters for months. Perhaps I am standing exactly where that store once was. Ivan holds me, but after a while, biting down on sobs, I shake loose from him. I cannot cry now; if I start, I'll never stop. I stare up into the peaceful-seeming, treacherous sky, perfectly blue except for a few feathery clouds, so much like the sky of that terrible morning. I crane my neck way back and look around. I see more sky, see the tallest skyscraper close by to the south and fix my gaze on it, because it, at least, is *there, up there,* solid, visible, massive, true.

But the towering building begins to sway, and then it begins to lean. Yes, it is swaying. It is leaning. It is leaning further in one direction now. My heart stops. "Oh no!"

"What *is* it?" Ivan panics at the expression on my face. He grabs me.

"It's falling!"

"What's falling? Are *you* falling?"

I point up to the top of the skyscraper. My head is spinning now. "It's happening *again*!"

"Nothing is falling," he says gently. "Nothing is happening." He cranes his neck into the same position as mine. "Okay, I get it. It's how you're standing." Shielding his eyes from the sun with his flattened hand, he peers intently upward. "An optical illusion. When the clouds are moving quickly in one direction, you feel that the building is leaning the other way." He looks me over now, to check that I have not freaked out any more—but how can he tell, if I am frozen in terror?—then he looks back up. "I can see it, what you're seeing. Whoooa!" He seems to stumble backwards and catch himself.

I know the building cannot be falling because if it were falling it would have fallen by now. We all know how long it takes for a skyscraper to tumble down in this city, out of the blue. That is my logic. So Ivan and his explanation must be right. Sure, now I can see it myself, the way the clouds move, the optical trick. But it is too late to reverse the deep terror of my first impression: it has already silenced me, stopped my heart, halted the blood in its circulation through my veins. I stagger down to the street in a state of suspended animation.

AS WE WALK east along Fulton Street, my inner voice is quiet, I cannot will it to speak new thoughts, and yet my body moves forward, sights register on my optic nerves, in fact all of my senses are now in a state of heightened alert. My adrenal gland must be churning out hormones like there's no tomorrow. I am pure nerve, flight-and-fight, a high-wire act without a net; for several minutes I am on emergency cruise control, there but not there. Ivan knows better than to talk now, but even when he tries to hug me or hold hands, I am frozen, a zombie. I have joined the living dead. We head toward the Brooklyn Bridge like the gray-ash-covered zombies who fled in indescribable panic from the advance of exploding towers in the debris-swirled dark that hellish morning; one foot in front of the other, each step bringing safety a few inches closer, if safety would ever exist again. We pass the apartment building where my mother lived for many years; a wide, hand-printed GOD BLESS AMERICA banner hangs from a series of windows—I count up—on the seventh floor. From her eleventh floor my mother *oohed* and *ahhed* over water views, over freighters and tug boats and tall ships. We pass the pizza place where she got her spinach calzones. We continue along the route of the guy who picked through trash with a wheelbarrow in the middle of many nights, singing at the top of his lungs. I am unable to resist the pummeling of memories; random glimpses of my own past rain down and cover me like a coating of gray dust: the smelly forays to the fish market, a concert on the pier, an argument on the pier—Was it with Daniel? With David? We made up and kissed passionately afterward; I remember the sludgy, roiled look of the water below as we kissed and I remember the kiss but not *who* I kissed, nor do I re-call the subject of our quarrel. And now onward along South Street and skirting Chinatown, a chaotic, black-and-white newsreel from my youth, visits with cousins who lived on Park Row, a restaurant buffet with eel, we approach the bridge. I don't know where to put myself, my old scattering of New York life, in this picture where the towers have been erased. And then we start onto the bridge like once I started with Daniel, covered then not in ashy dust but in the manic blanket of new true love, reciting half-remembered Whitman together, making up lines when memory faltered. And not so many months later I was deeply in love again with David, and across the bridge again with this other man, this one with hair as long as mine, kissing our way to Brooklyn, and suddenly I dropped Daniel. One day we were happily together, the next day I was gone—oh shit—I shudder now, I groan.

"What?" says Ivan, worried about me again.

Voice returns, raspy. "I walked across this bridge with a boyfriend named Daniel. We were living together and one day I went off with David. Just like that. I cringe thinking of the hurt I inflicted."

Ivan listens.

"So callous, so cruel. In my youth."

"And now? In your old age?"

"And now, too, I suppose, but I think I am more aware. At least I tell myself I am more aware."

Ivan takes my hand. I let him.

Ivan and I step farther and farther from lower Manhattan where I loved men and left men, eventually three of them, and the bridge shudders from traffic and wind, and we go all the way across the river, one foot in front of the other, silent, terrified, to Brooklyn Heights. As planned, at the midpoint of the bridge, David and I met up with his friends, clean-cut Isaac the architect with his obsession about doors and Franny the math teacher with long blond hair— well-brushed, glistening, classy long blond hair, unlike my supposedly artsy long black hair pulled artlessly into an unkempt ponytail. We walked with them to Montague Street and went down the side streets of brownstones in the Heights, examining every door, thanks to good-natured Isaac all of us suddenly experts in antique carvings and knockers and ornate paneling and stained glass. I see how beautiful they are still, those doors, and even amid this onslaught of unstoppable past, those same doors rear up into the present.

I would like to hold on to some of it, I would like to grab at least a few pieces of this memory barrage and look at them more carefully, but they rush away, they vaporize, only to be replaced by more fragments.

On the way to the Promenade we pass Uncle Joe's building, where his bookcases overflowed with the thousands of volumes he had read through decades of self-education. None of that generation, my family's stoic bulwark, went to college. And yet he knew everything, my Uncle Joe, he could do everything, it seemed, until he could do nothing as Aunt Helen wasted away from cancer, the view of bridge and skyline that she adored until her dying day finally haunting him, chiding him for his uselessness. And afterward I would visit him now and then, I would water Helen's droopy plants now and then, go out with him now and then to the Chinese restaurant he tried to still like in the midst of unending inconsolability, General Tso's chicken and sweet-and-sour soup and shrimp fried rice giving begrudging sustenance but none of their former pleasure. Ivan and I pass the restaurant and the General Tso's chicken and shrimp fried rice, we pass the ghost of my Uncle Joe, who died a decade ago, sitting at a table by the window bemoaning the state of the world, and the ghost of myself, across from him, chasing grains of rice around my plate with chopsticks as I listen to his tirades and agree.

Ivan and I stroll along the promenade, staring across to Manhattan. We stop. The towers are not there. For a second or two I can see them so clearly in my mind's eye, I can see the people standing in the jagged slits of windows above the flames and billowing smoke, some with legs straddling the sills, heads hanging out gasping for air, crowds behind pushing, pushing . . .

Then I try to see their absence: a distinct absence of towers, a distinct absence of people in them. But the rest of the city closes effortlessly into the lower space where they used to be, while the open sky reasserts itself at the higher levels. What is no longer there across the harbor is no longer visible. I cannot see the absence of towers. And why am I surprised? After the airborne debris had cleared in September, after the last swirls of smoke and cascades of dust and blizzards of ash and grizzly confetti that might have still, genie-like, conjured up a former presence had finally dissipated; after it had all settled on windowsills and tabletops and sidewalks and roofs and skin, inside lungs, on every exposed and unexposed surface built and sprouted and born for miles and miles—how could the absence of the towers be discerned? It could not. We continue. Makeshift shrines and memorials cling along the fencing here, too, with ribbons and flowers, pictures and poems, candles burned and unburned. A large framed photograph of what the view used to be hangs on the fence: the skyline with towers.

On the subway back to Manhattan, posters stare down at us and instruct: Feel free to feel better. New York gives permission to feel, exactly what Boston withholds. But may I now also feel free to feel worse?

Fifteen

You might think you can't mix up all these things, but you can. She thinks she teaches them writing, teaches them logic and flow. But does it make sense, anymore, to make sense?

ON A LATE gray winter afternoon, the sky prepares to let loose another assault of thick snow. I sit at my desk, sorting through class notes and slides, when a stirring in my doorway catches my attention. I am annoyed to be interrupted but look up. Smiling down toward me is a handsome black face, beard flecked with gray. I know this man, but who is he? I smile back, waiting for my slow brain to flip through its myriad associations. And then I realize it is Hassan, Ibrahim's friend, who has stepped out of the world of the Arabian hospital nights, where I last saw him two months ago, and into this other universe, my office, where I would not expect him.

"*Salaam*, Erika," he says.

"Oh no," I blurt, before he says another word. My feelings fly around every which way like swarms of dormant insects suddenly prodded from the hive with a hostile jab.

"Yes," says Hassan.

I try to hold in my tears. "He is gone? When?"

"Yesterday morning, Abu Dhabi time. Safiya's sister-in-law called me."

"Was he home?"

"No, in hospital. It was better for the children that way, at the end." We hug. Then Hassan sits down. "Safiya wanted you to know, but she could not bear calling you."

"Of course not." From the windows in my office, Hassan and I watch large snowflakes begin to fall. "And Mahmoud? Any news? Any word from the lawyer?"

Hassan shakes his head. "The lawyer is afraid he was taken out of the country for interrogation."

"You mean Guantanamo?"

"Nobody really knows, but we hear Afghanistan, we hear maybe Egypt or Syria."

We sit in silence for many minutes. The snowflakes, falling more steadily, seem to say everything that can possibly be said. Eventually Hassan hugs me again and leaves.

The next day at the same time the two sisters appear in my doorway, the engineer and the anthropology student, daughters of Gabriel, with a box of chocolates. The day after that, the Lost Boys bring flowers.

Sixteen

❖

Actually she liked it when everything came to a grinding halt, when the relentless fiction of constant striving, constant strife had to stop. For a few days, the world could pause and think. It could breathe. She imagined a whole month like this, every year. She named it Remembruary.

AT THE FIRST meeting of the advanced seminar class in the new semester, each student talks about her topic and the embryonic first draft that's required at the start. Sam clicks away on his laptop, even as students speak. His email signal pings over and over again.

It's Alice's turn. "My tentative title is this: *Household food distribution practices: women and children last?*" Her voice takes an upward lilt, in the way so many voices of her generation do. She has completed all her coursework except this seminar, and had continued to vacillate with topics for a semester while she did an internship in Ecuador. Now she's back for the home stretch.

"Catchy," says Sanford. "That's a catchy title."

Marianne says, "I like the take-off on women and children first." She observes confusion in Vinh's face and Carmen's. "In this country we say that for, like, getting into lifeboats. 'Women and children first!'"

"When do Americans get into lifeboats?" asks Fawzia, already starting out as this class's reality checker.

Alice cuts in. "Wait, I'm not done. There's a subtitle: *a cross-national gendered nutritional perspective on maternal-child health, comparing rural regions in southern Ethiopia, western Pakistan, the Philippines, and Ecuador.* That's the title. The first draft is not really finished, but I figured I better stop once I hit thirty pages."

I have an urge to duck under the table, but this is when I'm supposed to speak. I'm the teacher. I'm one of the teachers. "It's an interesting and potentially very useful topic. But it's awfully . . . errrr . . . *ambitious* for a twenty-page paper," I say. "Even if you did only one of those things, that is, took a gendered perspective, or did a nutritional analysis and applied it to women's health, or applied it to children's health, any one of those in any one country would more than fill twenty pages. Could you even find comparable data on four such different regions with such different cultural practices, let alone do them all justice in twenty pages? Can you rethink the scope?"

"Maybe just two or three of the regions?" asks Alice. "Like maybe do either Pakistan or the Philippines, not both; they're both in Asia anyway."

We have a long pause.

"Sam?" I ask, finally. "Do you have suggestions for Alice?"

Sam stops thumping at his keyboard. He purses his lips into a confident smile. "If you're really looking for something cutting-edge about women, then you couldn't do better than to tackle prevention of gender inequity as countries plan for smallpox immunization: it's one thing if women and girls eat last, or are the last to get sent to school; you're right that those kinds of inequity are not good for women, obviously, but let me tell you, it's altogether fatal if women aren't vaccinated in equal proportion to men before smallpox hits."

After a few seconds of confusion, Alice's face lights up. "Ensuring gender equity in smallpox vaccination," she says slowly. "I could keep the general framework of analysis, but add the smallpox vaccination angle as the primary focus."

"There you go." Sam's smile broadens and he returns to his typing. Students exchange glances with one another, suppress smirks. Vinh's head tilts sideways as he sends me a look of sympathy. I am speechless.

"But there *is* no smallpox," blurts Fawzia. "If nobody has it, how can it be fatal? Why write about a hypothetical disease?"

Sam's typing stops again. His eyes narrow and turn darkly grouchy. I know his next move will be not to respond to Fawzia's question but to rail against it. Before he can start, I say: "Moving right along—of course we'll be returning to every topic in detail in the coming weeks—please, Michael, tell us a little about *yours.*"

This works. Michael speaks. Sam doesn't. Alice, now on fire, also begins clattering on her laptop while Michael elaborates on his guinea worm eradication topic. It's hard not to listen carefully as he details for us the way the long worms start poking out of the human body through the skin, usually the legs. But Alice and Sam are having a speed-typing contest. Distracted by their fingertip frenzy, the rest of us can barely sustain our guinea worm repulsion. I cannot tell Alice to stop because I cannot thereby implicitly reprimand Sam in front of the whole class. I will need to nab him before he rushes out. But when the session ends, Alice pushes her open laptop in front of me. "Here's my new topic," she says proudly.

I read it aloud. "*The implications of household food distribution practices for smallpox vaccination strategies in resource-constrained countries: women and children last? A cross-national gendered nutritional perspective on dealing with bioterrorism, comparing rural regions in Asia, Ecuador, and southern Ethiopia.*" Once I've spit it out, I'm speechless. My mouth hangs open just a bit as I turn to her.

"I like the narrower focus, too," she says, as if I have commented. "Thanks for the suggestions, you guys. Thanks, Sam!" she calls out after him, as he scurries out the door. "This is gonna be a great class," Alice declares. "I love it already."

"THERE'S COFFEE CAKE." It's not even eight o'clock, and Toby is already in my doorway. "I made coffee, and Tina made us a coffee cake. Apple-walnut coffee cake. I don't know about you, but that's definitely *my* favorite." This time he sets down a paper plate on my desk with a thick slice of cake, like an offering.

"Thanks, Toby," I say. I do not say, Soon we will all be as round and doughy as you and your father. I do not ask, Where do you hide the ax? I do not say, Must I keep keeping your secrets? Or just, Please, leave me alone—better yet, go find a job somewhere else. Wouldn't all this go away if *you* went away? My relationship with Toby is defined by what I *don't* say now, more than what I *do*. Which I realize may not be altogether fair to *him*. But who started it, anyway?

I pick up a paper, as if about to turn my attention to reading.

"Aren't you gonna eat the cake?"

"It's too early, Toby. I'll have it later, with coffee."

"I can get you a cup of coffee now if you want."

"No thanks, Toby. I already had one cup at home. It's too soon now for a second cup."

He takes a gulp from his smiley-face mug. "Tina only drinks tea, so I don't make coffee at home in the morning. Just here. I don't start on coffee until I'm here. Tina's already up drinking tea and feeding the baby when I'm taking a shower and getting dressed. She might even be making applesauce already, or doing a scrapbook all over the table. The kitchen is already hers. She runs a pretty tight ship. She'll be giving the baby a bath at like 7:09 on the nose every day. I just come straight here."

I do not say, Please spare me the details of your domestic life. But it occurs to me that these early morning conversations with me must now be, in a way, part of his domestic life. He arrives at the office lonely. He gets here in the morning full of the same unspoken anxieties and insecurities that he must have gone to sleep with the night before. *Leave me alone*, I think.

I wave a sheaf of papers in the air. "Toby, I come in this early so I can read papers before the noise and interruptions get started on this floor."

He looks a little panicked, then flashes a big, open smile. "Yeah. Sorry. I just wanted to tell you the latest. There's an eight-hour difference. I see Frances's emails when I get in. All the emails from Kenya."

I sigh. "So?"

"So, the girl we fired. Bertha. She took pictures. So now I see the squalor these people live in. I thought you'd want to know that

I see it better now, how poor they are. The shacks they live in. The filthy streets." He shudders. "I get it now. It's not pretty."

I am silent.

"And one of the mothers is a hooker."

I remain silent.

"There's a picture of her, coming out of a pathetic little bar with a man. It's practically falling down, this bar. Some planks of wood hammered together."

I wonder, did Mr. Edwards bludgeon her first? Or suffocate her? Or did he just start hacking away with the ax right from the start?

"Another picture shows her standing in a . . . well, a pose." Toby strikes a pose himself, hands on hip, one hip pushing up higher than the other, head thrown back, face smiling upward. Then he collapses back into big, hunched, rounded Toby, the unbaked loaf. "You know. Looking for men. It's disgusting."

"You don't have to open all the pictures, just because she sent them."

He doesn't hear me, he's so into it. "And another one, with . . . with a man. Probably they're doing it. Standing up against a wall." I can't tell if the weird, slightly manic look sweeping quickly across Toby's face is revulsion or arousal. It lasts only a second, then disappears.

"Delete the pictures, Toby."

"But she sent them to me. To everyone on the project list. Bertha, the girl who screwed up the project sent them to the whole list. There's gotta be a reason."

"She's pissed because she got fired. Delete them."

"She says the woman in the pictures is from one of our households. I don't know if we should believe her, but Frances can't go into the slum at night to check it out. It's not safe. But Frances totally doesn't care anyway. She says this is what people have to do to get by. That's ridiculous. Yesterday I happened to get my shots for yellow fever, typhoid, and hepatitis."

"You *happened* to get shots for tropical diseases?"

"Yup. I'm set to go. Like, if this head of the household is really out on the streets, somebody better step in."

"No intervention," I say. "Remember?"

"I understand, but think of the poor little children in the house." I allow silence. "Little children could get hurt."

The little boy with the throbbing heartbeats and the itch at the tip of his nose, silent on the stand, tugs at me. I resist. He sees that his father's mouth twists back and forth from grin to frown to grin again, movements as involuntary as the boy's own twitching nose and rumbling stomach. He can't tell what his father's changed face means. The boy did just what he was told: he said nothing. But maybe his father is ashamed of *him* (though he had thought it should be the other way around). Maybe everyone is ashamed of him. The little boy looks up at me with soft, pleading eyes. Am I ashamed of him, too? No. I am afraid of him. I don't want him here. I push him away, letting my silence go on longer.

Finally Toby aims one of his more penetrating, point-making stares at me. Then suddenly he lightens up and smiles.

"Okay. I know you're thinking. Tell me what you think."

"I think you ought to stay away from prostitutes, Toby."

His faux-friendly eyes quickly narrow into beady squints. They are creepy eyes, his father's eyes. They are where'd-I-leave-the-ax eyes. "What did you say?"

I say it again. "Stay away from prostitutes, Toby."

He turns bright red. "Why are you saying that? Why are you saying that to me? Like that?"

"Why do you think?"

He stews for a few moments in his redness. "No, really, why?"

I snap right back: "Really, Toby. Why do you think?" I am not going to say what he thinks I might say. Whatever that is. Two can play this game.

"Shit." He turns and leaves.

I close my door. I lock it. I banish the boy in the yellow sweater from my mind and toss the coffee cake into the trash.

WE ARE RESPONDING to a page of a draft.

"The sentence is fifteen lines long," says Vinh. "By time I get to end, I forget beginning."

"I see so much jargon piled on—empowerment, resource-constrained, marginalized—I'm confused," says Fawzia. "I'm not sure those words mean the same thing to me as they mean to the writer."

Michael tries to put a positive spin on his reaction. "It seems to me that about six different ideas are getting started in this one sentence. I think I'll be interested in the ideas, but not all jammed together like this."

"Good!" I step in. "You are getting very good at using I-statements to describe the experience of reading, rather than going on the attack. Was that helpful, Carmen?"

Carmen is writing rapidly on her own page. "Yes! Yes!"

"Okay. Even though things occur simultaneously," I tell the class, "in writing you can only narrate them sequentially, linearly. You cannot say everything at the same time. Wouldn't it be nice to be able to write on a round globe so that you see everything in one piece no matter which way you turn it or look at it? But the written world is flat. We can't write on a multi-dimensional sphere. We can't write everything in one sentence, try as we might to cram it all together so that the connectedness imposed by a sentence structure stands in for simultaneity. But you *can* tell the reader, explicitly, that all these factors or events are simultaneous or intricately connected, that one does not exist without the other. No grammatical or syntactical arrangement automatically denotes this coexistence, but we do make abundant use of clues and cues, announcements and summaries and explicitness in taking the reader through our thinking."

"In addition and moreover," says Vinh. "Furthermore, too."

"On the other hand," says Carmen.

"However," adds Blaise.

"At the same time," says Fawzia.

"We will explore several reasons. First, second, and third."

"Others have indicated."

"For example."

"However."

"Despite these limitations."

"Finally, we will conclude with recommendations for further research," says Alice.

"However." Blaise's refrain is also the prelude to silence. They are done.

"Okay, that's sort of the idea," I say.

Sam looks up from his computer screen, arching his eyebrows at me.

I take a big breath. "And sometimes you have to admit you can't address the whole chain of factors, however inseparable every link seems to be from every other link, however much we know that the social and cultural and political and clinical and bacterial and viral and economical and occupational and environmental and meteorological and pharmaceutical and geographical and chemical and genetical and nutritional and spiritual and sexual and textual and educational and global and local"— I take another big breath— "impinge directly on the subject at hand (and always in any health issue they all always impinge, don't they?)—you can come clean and say you're only going to write about a certain defined fraction of the whole."

"That was a much too long sentence right there," says Sam.

"I know. That's my prerogative as a teacher. Yours, too."

"Are you sure you want to set that terrible example?" he asks.

"At least she didn't write it down," says Alice. "Like I would."

"But it was funny," says Vinh. "It was on purpose very funny sentence."

"Thank you, Vinh." I think I am falling in love with Vinh.

"I don't believe *genetical* is actually a word," says Sam. "I believe *genetic* is correct."

"Thank you, Sam." I go on. "You can tell your reader that you recognize the interconnectedness of a whole range of factors, but that some of it—even most of it—is *beyond the scope of this paper*. Once you hammer out a clear problem statement, you'll know better what's in and what's out."

So that particular learning objective is finally covered. I wait to see how it plays out. And soon I know.

Alice's topic morphs again, this time into the readiness of developing country health systems for preventing and containing smallpox, with Ecuador as the focal case. It is even harder for me to imagine smallpox unleashed by terrorists in downtown Quito than in downtown Manhattan, where terrorism has already been unleashed but where I still can't envision smallpox. But Alice has spent time in Ecuador. She seems to believe, perhaps with a little prodding by another member of the faculty, that the topic is apt. Her years' obsession with gender equity has withered away into a footnote. And inevitably, in the fifth revision of her problem statement since the start of the course, this disclaimer appears: "While studies of health system infrastructure and preparedness have been done in Brazil as well as Ecuador, Brazil is beyond the scope of this paper."

"But *why?*" I ask Alice. "Why *not* Brazil? Usually when we say something is beyond the scope, we're referring to a conceptual area, not a geographical area. You can tell us why you're focusing on Ecuador specifically, but if relevant studies of comparable situations in Brazil would shed light on the situation in Ecuador, then to impose a geographical boundary may not make sense."

"But I've never been to Brazil," says Alice.

"THERE'S BROWNIES." TOBY is in my doorway again, standing up straight again, rebounding again. Nothing I say drives him away; in fact, the more I provoke him, the more resolve he seems to invest in returning, all smiley-faced and chipper. He's like a puppy that gets kicked, whimpers away, licks his wounds, and then comes back for more, tail wagging. Today I got to my office after nine, when I knew Fiona would already be around and Fred would be in the internships office and the receptionist would be at her desk, too.

"You're kind of late," he says.

"Toby, I'm faculty. Remember? I can set my own hours. As long as I'm here for classes and office hours and meetings, there's no such thing as late."

"I know, but you're later than usual."

"So?"

"There's brownies. This is the *third* time I've come to tell you, but you weren't here before. You weren't here at your usual time." Now he looks seriously pissed, not chipper, and his tone is a tad whiney, especially the way he emphasizes *third*.

"Toby, just accept it. You won't be able to set your watch by me. Anyway, now I'm on a diet."

He laughs. "Yeah, maybe, but not for long. Wait 'til you see Tina's brownies in the kitchen. They're the greatest. I guarantee you won't be able to resist."

I give him an arched eyebrow. "We'll see."

He slouches there, one round shoulder against the edge of my doorway, watching me as I remove folders from my briefcase, then take papers from a folder.

"Toby, I have to prepare for a ten o'clock class. Will you excuse me?"

"Just don't forget to get a brownie before they're all gone." He stays put.

I sigh. "Okay, I get it. You want to tell me something. What's the news today?"

He grins his best smiley-face grin and stands up straight. "Nussbaum's sending me to Kenya for a couple of weeks."

"Oh yeah?"

"Isn't that great? He can't make it himself so he's sending me to Nairobi to straighten things out. I finally get a chance to implement my skill set on the ground. I'm gonna turn that project around in no time."

"How about Tina and the baby? Will they manage without you for a couple of weeks?"

"They'll manage just fine. They always do. Not a day goes by Tina doesn't manage well without me."

Does he know what he has just said to me?

"And has Frances signed off?"

He gives a dismissive little snort. "Nussbaum's gonna talk to her today. It's his call, y'know, not hers."

He stands there waiting. He stands unusually tall and straight expecting my approval and admiration and congratulations. His hair is parted a little too far to the left today, just like Mr. Edwards's hair used to be, setting a short, annoying cowlick into space.

I rummage through my papers for a minute. Finally I say, "I don't think it's such a good idea, Toby. To be perfectly honest, I don't think you should be the one to go to Nairobi."

His shoulders fall, the tension holding up his facial muscles lets go, too. His default face is a blank. He bites his lower lip for a few seconds, he keeps himself together. "Are you going to tell me why?"

"You know why," I say.

"No I don't," he says. "I really don't." He slumps against the doorjamb. A minute goes by and neither of us speaks. A ten-year-old boy sits on the stand, silent. Quaking. Each of his heartbeats is like a truck backfiring, and each boom startles him anew, wakes him from a bad dream into which he plunges again only to be startled a second later by the next insistent, terrified boom of life in his chest. He cycles in and out of this nightmare, just sitting there, eyes open, boom after boom. Second after second. Minute after minute. All is silent, even the questions he doesn't listen to, doesn't answer, doesn't know the answers to. Where was he? What did he see? The people staring at him are very small and far away, as if he looks at them through a telescope held backwards.

Then he says, "Are you going to tell Nussbaum not to let me go?"

I look straight into Toby's face. "Should I? Should I tell him something?"

He turns and leaves, slamming my door closed behind him.

Seventeen

❖

She has a dream that the dead have trouble letting go of the living. She always thought it was the other way around. A man is standing close behind her; she is quite sure it is Ibrahim though she does not see him and she does not turn around to check. He latches onto her from behind, his grip on her back so tight it pushes her breath away. Then he circles his arms around her abdomen and squeezes, squeezes harder, she can no longer breathe at all. She knows this is not a hug, it is not a sexual embrace, it is not even affectionate: it is sheer panic, his panic and now her panic, he is squeezing her, she is sure he is squeezing her to death, a drowning man pulling her down with him. But suddenly the squeeze, the holding-on-for-dear-life lightens—"I am going now." He whispers those last words closely into her left ear. She breathes, finally, then wriggles around sideways and sees that he has—what?—he has let go. Died. That word also sneaks up from behind and frightens her. She somehow sees he has died but she doesn't see him. She knows he is dead. She wakes herself up with a panicky jolt.

IVAN WON'T SPEND the night at my place. I can stay at his, and these days often do, but he has a thing about leaving my bed before daybreak, having drawn this particular line in the sands of our stop-and-go intimacy. So now he's at my place, in my bedroom, in my bed. We've had unusually intense lovemaking—somehow a spurt of renewal, a bigger joy, when (we think) we're not actually *in* love, when (we think) our bodies aren't *saying* anything of much

169

importance to one another. We are here; we are spent. Really spent. It was a long day even before our achy-kneed middle-aged acrobatics, me teaching a special faculty workshop, Ivan with an audit from the NIH. So we fall asleep, we sleep deeply, and it is not until nearly four o'clock in the morning when Ivan wakes and stirs, waking me, too. Only two more hours and he would be here through the night. I am curious: will he chuck it for this once and just roll over? Or will he panic and rush out?

I look into his face and immediately see that something is wrong, more wrong than four o'clock.

"Where am I?" he asks, his voice raspy, shaky, and strangely anxious.

"You're in my house." I see this is not registering anything and his face is pale. "My little house on the water. It's Tuesday night. Actually, it's Wednesday morning."

"The water?"

"In Quincy. On Dorchester Bay. Boston Harbor." He still looks confused. "The Atlantic Ocean. North America. Planet Earth."

"Okay, okay. I know I'm not on Mars, for God's sake." Still he looks unsettled. "And you're . . ." He does not intone a question, but he stops.

"Erika," I say. Something is *really* wrong here.

He seems to sigh with relief. "Yes, of course. Erika. I know who you are. But how did we get here?" He sits up straight. I sit up, too, and turn on the light.

"Ivan, what's the last thing you remember?"

He screws up his face in the effort to remember. "The auditor. The auditor was in my office, from NIH. The National Institutes of Health."

"Okay, good." That *was* yesterday.

"So what happened to him? How did I get *here*? What did we *do*?"

"You don't remember picking me up and having dinner at the Thai restaurant?" I hold my breath.

"No," he says forlornly.

"The drive in the rain, the detour when that section of Morrissey Boulevard that's always flooded was flooded?"

He frowns. "No."

"Ivan, the greatest sex we've ever had. On and on. You don't remember *that*?"

He shakes his head and shrugs. He looks down at his own belly, regards the fleshy rolls of middle age as if he is seeing *them* for the very first time.

"You'll have to take my word for it. You were superhuman." A stupid joke: really I am terrified. What if he never remembers anything? What if his mind disappeared overnight? Will I be stuck with him forever? Or will Anya take him? Why are these my immediate concerns, and not the medical threat itself, the possibility he has had a stroke?

His eyes seem blank. "Is this what they call amnesia? I don't remember a thing. Just the auditor."

He jumps out of bed, walks to the window, looks out. Stark naked, he makes a quick tour of the house. I pull on a robe and follow behind him at a respectful distance, turning on lights.

"Okay," he says, moving away the drapes to peer out the living room window at the view of the bay. "I know this place. We've been here before?"

171

"Ivan, it's my house."

"Of course." He looks at me, as if trying not to let on that he doesn't really recognize who I am. Even in the throes of amnesia, he's a gentleman.

He takes his own pulse, examines his eyes carefully in the mirror, palpates his carotid arteries, bonks his own knee to test his reflexes. "I seem to be all right." He puts on his shorts and tee shirt.

"Relax," I say, my voice high-pitched with fear. "It's just one of those weird things."

"It's not total amnesia," he says, a bit cheerier. "I know who *I am*." As he pulls on his trousers, he recites his phone number, his social security number, his address, his license plate number, his son's name and birth date. We both breathe a sigh of relief.

"Okay, on Saturday I visited Sergei and Rita and the baby in Amherst. Sunday, I worked in the office, getting ready for the audit. Monday, that was yesterday, the chairman—Nussbaum! Yes, evil little Nussbaum!"—he chuckles—"helped me review all the reports, the budgets. Tuesday—no, *that* was yesterday, wasn't it?—the auditor came. It took too long but it went all right. He left—yes, now I remember!—he left just before six, I saw him to a cab. A yellow cab with an Internet ad on top." Now he smiles.

"Good," I cheer him on. "It's coming back."

"An ad for broadband access. Cute, with that animated logo thing smiling in the corner." He laughs triumphantly.

I'm starting to worry that whatever this phenomenon is, it means he's remembering the minutia, the trivial details, without the bigger picture. But not to worry.

"I closed up the office, I talked for a few minutes with Sam about his new smallpox article, I got my car." He pauses. "It was Tuesday, Tuesday the eighteenth."

I sigh my own quiet, private sigh of relief. But not so fast.

He clutches his chin with one hand, deep in thought. He scratches his head. He looks at me, embarrassed, and shrugs. "I'm sorry, but after that, it's a blank."

I toss my head back. "Don't worry. It was just another one of our forgettable evenings."

"No, no. Please don't be hurt."

"Ivan, I'll be very happy if you just see a doctor today and make sure you're okay. Okay?"

"Yes, I will. Everything *is* coming back, you know. It's just taking a little time, but it's all getting sharper. The fuzziness is gone. At least up to that one point. And you, *of course*. You're back to me in complete 3-D." He grabs my hand, pulls me close to him, kisses me on the forehead. "Thank you," he whispers. "Whoever you are."

"Ivan!" I shriek.

He laughs. "That's a joke!" he says. "See, my sense of humor is back, too."

"Ivan, it's not *funny*!"

He chuckles to himself as he puts on his socks.

"It's some sort of fugue, there's got to be an explanation," I say. "Please have breakfast. Let me drive you to work."

"Oh no!" he is buttoning up his shirt, tying his shoelaces. Physical coordination is obviously normal. "I'm okay, really. I'm fine!"

Except that you've completely forgotten the best night we ever had, I think, but I don't say it. The man has enough to worry about. I insist that he call me when he gets to school, and he does. Everything feels almost normal again, he says. But he assures me he has an appointment with his doctor at eleven.

After my class that afternoon, he ducks into my office, circumspect as usual, closing the door quickly and speaking in a low voice, nearly a whisper, as if no one in the department has guessed about our dalliance. So far all the tests are fine.

More tests, more results follow. And everything checks out. Nothing neurological, nothing cardiological, nothing hematological, nothing at all is wrong. By the end of the week when all the tests are interpreted by a host of the best specialists in this town full of specialists, we know he is definitely his same old self. There is no physical explanation. And he remembers absolutely everything— *except that night* when we got too close and flew into the flame.

I AM UNMOORED, adrift. Seas are rough. There is a small craft advisory, and if ever there was a small craft, it is me. I have made Ivan my anchor, but if the anchor is just as detached and buoyant and unhinged as I am, bobbing along wherever the current takes it, where does that leave me, the vessel which had needed to be held steady in one place?

I try to help him pack, but I have long been a clothes-roller and he is an unapologetic folder. Despite my protests, he stacks up his neatly creased shirts on one side of the suitcase, trousers and a sweater on another. It will be cold in Geneva, where he has meetings with experts at the World Health Organization. It will be very hot in Tanzania, where he'll give a keynote address at a big conference and take part in several plenary panels, then help evaluate a World Bank project. I used to envy him his many invitations, his frequent travels, his prominence in global circles. But this is his first trip by air since the attacks and I am not envying him this trip; why envy a world traveler in this world? He is a little nervous but pretends not to be, and brushes off any suggestion that things have changed, flight-wise.

"But the airport is spooky, half-empty," I remind him.

"Good. That means more room for *me*. Anyway, this is the safest time it has ever been to fly, with so many precautions."

"Gun-toting marshals pose as clueless tourists in the seat next to you in coach. That's *safe?*"

He shrugs. "It's nothing." He tucks a pair of shoes into a cloth sack. "Anyway, I'm more likely to get killed in a car wreck in Tanzania than in any of the planes."

"Well that certainly puts my mind at ease." I frown at him. "What a relief."

I offer to search his carry-on bag and its toiletry case for illegal items, for clippers and files, scissors and knives, hammers, box-cutters, guns, cigarette lighters, explosives, and—God forbid!—tweezers.

"Do you even know what you've got in there? What about umbrellas? Pens? Suspenders and belts?"

"Those are all allowed."

"But why *aren't* they banned? Imagine the headline: Pilots overcome by pen-wielding terrorist. Why not? If tweezers could do it, why not a pen? Or how about a stewardess strangled with suspenders."

"I've never even worn suspenders."

"Captain hung by his belt. Crew knocked unconscious by heavy briefcase filled with teddy bears."

"Teddy bears? Innocent teddy bears?"

"A smack on the head with a hard-sided case—what difference does it make, what's inside? The outside could kill you. Ban briefcases. Ban suitcases. Why not?"

"Ban people," he says. "That would do it."

"Good idea. If you see a suggestion box at Logan, remember to put that in."

I grope my way around the inner corners of his carry-on bag and right away put my hand on a Swiss Army knife.

"Uh-uh, nothing doing." I dangle the contraband in front of his face.

"But that's my corkscrew, my paté spreader, my sausage slicer!"

"Too bad. You'll have to check it."

Inside the toiletries case I find a toothbrush, toothpaste, soap, shampoo, aspirin, vitamins. How boring. I unzip a small compartment—ah, now we're cooking. Nail clippers and disposable razors hide there. I take them out. I unzip another small compartment: insect repellent, stain remover packets, condoms.

Condoms. He packed condoms.

True, condoms are still allowed on board after 9/11. Do I say anything? Or is it too crude, or even sad—perhaps pathetic?—to draw attention to his hygienic contingencies, to recognize that hope springs absurdly eternal. He will never pass up an opportunity; on the brink of sixty, he is still searching for true love, the real thing. It has been evident all along that *I'm* not the real thing, but apparently not even the young and brilliant and beautiful Anya quite fills the bill. Or else why condoms? I feel bad for Anya. For whom is he willing to use these? Will he wait until *she* insists, or will he initiate the protection himself during an annual rendezvous in Geneva or a sudden head-over-heels fling in Arusha or a quickie in Dar es Salaam? What is he protecting her (them) from, that he did not feel was necessary with me? Conception, perhaps. The yearly tryst, or the unknown woman, the woman-yet-to-be-met, is young enough to be pumping out eggs at a fertile clip. But maybe I have it backwards. He is only protecting himself, and protecting himself *from* her. (*From* them.) He was so sure that he would never have to protect himself from *me*.

A shirt in hand, he stops folding and stands completely still; from the corner of my eye I can tell that he looks at me poking and prodding in the depths of every compartment, examining the case. I see a broody frown settle over his face: he wonders if I have found his condoms, if I have put my finger right smack on his unquenchable thirst. But he says nothing; he must hold out a faint hope that I haven't noticed. And if I have, he's damned if he'll come clean; I will have to speak first.

Our eyes meet and hold one another, engaged but hiding, waiting, purposely expressionless. For a long moment, neither of us gives. Neither of us moves. Is this the moment of truth? Or is it the moment of out-loud deception? Or the moment of forgiveness? The moment of forfeit? It's like a multiple-choice exam, and I pick all of the above. But he picks none.

Zipping up the case, I smile and carefully set his clippers and scissors on top of the dresser next to the Swiss Army knife.

"Clippers, scissors, knife," I say. "Paper, scissors, rocks. You're a dangerous man."

"Whoops," he grins a crooked grin and runs his fingers through his hair, looking especially disheveled, especially endearing.

"Better me finding them than the guys at the airport," I say. "They would only confiscate them." I smile again. "You would have to buy them back on eBay." I move around the bed toward him and kiss him on the forehead. "Good night, sweet prince," I say. He follows me as I go into the hallway and put on my coat.

"You're leaving already?" He seems flummoxed.

"That's better, don't you think? You'll have a good night's sleep." He tries to hide his confusion. I kiss him again. "Please have a good trip. A safe journey. You'll have email, yes? So send me a message from somewhere."

He looks at me half-smiling, half-puzzled. "I'll write from Geneva, at least."

I kiss him one more time. And then I'm out the door.

Eighteen

❖

Some stories are just too hot to handle. You have to cool them off, break them up into little pieces and blow on them.

I KNOW THIS about how it started. At first, Monica loved the green around her, how it filled in all the space as far as she could see on the broad hillside, how the sun played lighter and darker greens. She swam in a vast sea of bright emerald tea bushes, which had already grown taller than her waist, and rode the waves along the curving rows. Even at first her fingers moved quickly and skillfully, plucking off the top leaves, spinning them in one motion into the huge sisal basket strapped to her back. A cool early morning breeze teased her skin; skittering fluffs of clouds softened the sun as it blazed low in the endless Kenya sky. At first Kennedy worked near her, moving faster than she did but somehow staying close. They did not speak, but it made her happy to catch sight of him from the corner of her eye.

Happy. *Furaha.* She did not think about happiness, she was not ever led to expect happiness, and though people she knew were often at peace and content, and at celebrations even exuberant, an expectation of happiness was not part of the worldview where she came from. The syllables of the word in any language rarely came together on her lips. But in these first hours on the Kericho plantation, Monica could be said to be happy. Of course even during that very first day, the basket grew heavier, the weighing point got farther and farther away, her fingers suffered cuts, insects bit her, the residue of sprays gave her headaches, the sun burned relentlessly. It was difficult work. Her whole body ached. Henry, their burly field boss, yelled at them if anyone so much as stood for a moment to stretch or rest. Still, she was young. She liked that she and Kennedy had found each other and found their way here and started a life. She could earn in a day more money than she ever had before. She had already learned her way around plants from the stubborn garden at home; now she was so dexterous, knowing, and intimate with *these* plants, she could pick nearly as much as Kennedy, though he was much bigger and faster. And he was proud of her for her skill; he called it her magic touch. He was very tall and clever, thin but sinewy and strong; his confidence did not depend on someone else's weakness.

So she had hope. She did not think about hope, she did not articulate particular hopes to herself and certainly she did not make lists, but Monica could be said to be hopeful. From their little room in the plantation barracks, surrounded by hundreds of exhausted workers, her laughter was distinct as it fluttered out into the deep night over the others' soft murmurs, shouts, and groans. Her buoyancy endured, as did Kennedy's fascination with her. By nightfall they were very tired and their muscles hurt, but they were also both healthy and strong, so they sat outside, back to back leaning against one another in the dark, and looked up at the millions and millions of brilliant stars splashed so wantonly through the depths of their sky. They breathed in the moist, warm perfume of tea plants and earth. They pressed their shoulders hard against one another. She laughed her buoyant laugh. They believed they were lucky. They did not compare their lives to anyone else's; there was nothing next to which to feel deprived, and everything was new. They were young and like young people everywhere dwelled in beginnings, not ends. They did not wish for a stop to their hard labor in the tea anymore than they would have wished for the end of these stars overhead.

How fast hope evaporates.

One day not long after Monica knew she was pregnant, Henry, their boss, told Kennedy to work a different section of the hill, far out of sight from Monica. Because she and Kennedy had moved along the curve of the hillside so quickly, nearly all the pluckers were out of sight today. Henry was from her tribe; her instinct was to trust him. The *real* bosses were in England, a few worked in offices in Nairobi, and men with more authority than Henry were all over the Kericho estate, too. Henry was an insignificant speck in the order of things. But Henry was the only boss they knew. He sniggered at the longing looks they cast each other as Kennedy, reluctant but without protest, went off with his basket. Monica stood motionless, frowning.

"Get back to work!" he ordered.

First she flinched. But then she said firmly, "I'm *working*!"

"On your own, you'll pluck more." His tone softened. "You're very good, you know," he said, coming closer to her. "You could be the best. I can make sure you get paid for more kilos." She backed away, but he moved faster. Before she knew what was happening, he had pushed her basket off her shoulder, spilling half a morning's precious leaves, knocked her to the ground, and pinned her down with his full weight, the scratchy undergrowth prickling through her thin clothes. She took a breath to scream, but he held one hand over her mouth as he groped under her skirt with the other. "You want to keep this job? Then shut up."

It did not take long. He left her lying there. She got up, straightened her clothes, threw up in the weeds, slung her basket over her shoulder, and began plucking again, slowly getting up to speed.

People in England and America would not miss any breakfast tea.

At the weighing station, he added five kilos to her total that day. The next day, panicked and queasy, she made sure to wear an extra cloth around her waist and to spread it out to keep from getting scratched. That day he added ten kilos. But he did not overtake her every day, and it seemed that whatever pleasure he took for himself was enhanced by keeping her unsure and scared. Sometimes he would just swagger past her, smiling. Always he kept Kennedy at a distance, and always he kept her off her guard. When the pregnancy began to show, the extra kilos at the weighing station and the extra shillings stopped. Henry's caresses, always few and brusque, became painful, his mounting of her an even heavier, more suffocating invasion, his thrusts a series of sharp, punishing taunts. Each time he took longer to finish, deliberately, she was sure, to hurt her more, to keep her longer from plucking and earning. Finally, disgusted by her belly, he sent her to work in the factory, on the line sorting leaves for processing, where she earned only half as much as on a normal plucking day. Working faster made no difference in the factory—the pay was always the same. Only going slower

182

would make a difference; she saw that sick women and old women got hell for losing speed.

She told Kennedy that pregnant women were always moved to the factory for light duty. For all either of them knew, that was true. And off the field, though she earned much less those last four months of her pregnancy, at least she never saw Henry anymore. The torture was over. For her. Now another pretty young woman would get it.

Kennedy never found out what Henry did. What she did. In the final weeks of the pregnancy when he claimed she was as big as a warthog, Kennedy went into the town some nights and drank beer. She never said a word, never asked a question.

The beautiful baby girl was born, unharmed. Monica went to church and thanked God. They named her Faith. Such a pretty name! Kennedy doted on her and stayed home at night again. After a little time, Monica was able to return to plucking with Faith tied to her back. She did not see Henry on the fields, and she heard he'd been sent away. (Not for raping women, said the other women pluckers who she talked to more now, but for out-and-out theft of money. They laughed in grim and knowing snorts. Oh, money! So much more valuable than *us*!) Another boss, loud and coarse and unusually ugly, was no doubt forcing himself on other women, but Monica's baby protected her. She was, visibly and with no regrets, used goods. She picked a little more slowly, she hung back with the bigger grouping of women, no longer venturing ahead by herself or with Kennedy. The baby became nearly as heavy a weight to carry as the full basket of tea leaves and screamed to be let down on her own two feet, long after she was walking and running everywhere else, unstoppable. But out among the plants, Monica kept Faith tied to her back as long as she possibly could, even when she was pregnant again.

By the time Gilbert the baby boy arrived, Kennedy had started to seem weaker. Thinner. Not sick, exactly, but not himself, exactly, either. Strange eruptions appeared on his skin. At times he coughed so hard and so long, she feared all his insides would pour out. But he kept working. He did not want to take off the hours or even, possibly, the days he would need to go to the clinic. A few times, that first year when he seemed not always himself, his daily weight of leaves failed to measure up, and he was sent to work in the factory or to do the weeding with children and old women, until he got stronger again. Then he would become surly at home in their room, the same room from year to year to year; he became resentful. He was not an old woman, he grumbled; he was not a child.

But for a couple of years at least he always got stronger again, if never quite as strong as he was the last time he got stronger. In long spurts, he would pluck nearly as much as he used to, he might sing as he worked, he would take Monica in his arms. But then (after the third baby died) he stopped getting stronger again and only got weaker, coughing all night long. He thrashed in bed, drenched in fevered sweats. His body shriveled more and more— how he once looked sideways is how he began to look frontward. Though the little girl was supposed to be in school, sometimes they took her with them and let her pluck; she was tall and could reach the topmost leaves. At night Monica cried silently, bathing Faith's scratched and swollen arms and legs in tepid water, but for a while, at least the child's help kept up Kennedy's daily harvests, so he was not sent off to light duty, to be poorly paid and mocked.

For a while longer, a short while, he only weeded. He sat on the wet ground where the new tea plants were growing low, scooting along on his bottom to yank at weeds here and there, silent. But one day he could not get out of bed at all, and that's where he stayed, soiling himself and mumbling incoherently, in and out of consciousness. It was already too late to take him to his village. In two weeks he was dead. Holding tightly to little Gilbert's hand, Faith ran with the boy to find Monica plucking on the hillside to tell her. She finished her section, then asked for permission to leave.

Her voice quivered as she spoke to the boss. "Kennedy has been called home by God."

Suddenly she wished he had never been given that name, the name of a man who had died much too young. Instead of being the blessing once intended, the name had become a curse.

Kennedy's older brother in Nakuru expected to marry her; that was the way things were done. But when he told her at the funeral, Monica knew she could no longer do things the way they were done. Her sister Mary had moved with her family to Nairobi a year or two before; Monica decided to join them. It would mean losing everything, others told her. But what was everything? Not the love of her parents, who were also dead. Who else was left, only those who might shun her? Without Kennedy, without land or home of her own, Monica had nothing to lose. She had a few shillings saved from her last pay on the tea estate. Some worn cloths and clothes, a few utensils and a cooking pot, a broken doll that Faith and Gilbert had both outgrown, a dog-eared Bible, a hoe. To her, the reasons she should throw herself on the mercies of Kennedy's brother were the same reasons she might as well try her fortunes elsewhere. She believed that she and her children could start life again in Nairobi, too. Again, she felt a cautious, unarticulated surge of hope.

She was still strong in body and spirit. It was 1996. It would never have occurred to her, to anyone, that *she* had been the one to infect *him*. He had died first, after all.

Nineteen

❖

Now she's much more reconciled to total annihilation. In fact, she's starting to think it's not such a bad idea. If she can just get a few things done beforehand.

MICHAEL ANNOUNCES TO the class that his topic has changed. He has switched from the guinea worm problem in Togo to preparing for smallpox bioterrorism in Togo.

Fawzia says, "But people *have* guinea worms in Togo. Who has smallpox?"

"The worms are close to eradication anyway," says Michael. "Let's face it: guinea worms are the past. Smallpox is the future."

"But smallpox has *already* been eradicated," says Fawzia. "Completely."

"I liked the guinea worms," says Vinh, smiling.

Alice shudders, arms crossing her chest, hugging herself. "Ugh. Coming out through your *skin*? Are you serious?"

Vinh keeps smiling. "I liked that in my lifetime I would read that guinea worm problem is gone forever, and I will remember my classmate who helped win the fight."

"The world is changing so fast," Michael says to Vinh. "The fights are different now. We have to take chances to keep up with it all."

"Well," says Alice, "I happen to like that your topic now overlaps with mine. We can share sources."

"But you can't possibly finish before the end of the semester if you switch topics now," I say.

"I don't mind taking an incomplete. I'm okay with that." He bares his teeth in a confident grin.

There's nothing we can do to stop him. I move the discussion, the beginning-of-class check-in and update, to the next student. Week after week, this is how we wait for Sam to show up.

"I'm stuck," sighs Lena. "Paralyzed. I found a few successes in other countries, how to reach the intravenous drug users, get them into the HIV programs, improve addiction treatment, protect confidentiality, give access to sterile needles, too, in a way so they don't fear arrest. I know exactly what to propose." She frowns and sighs, tossing back her mane of frizzy red hair as she launches into a dialog with herself. "But who in Kazakhstan would do this? The government? Never. Even if there was money or resources. There isn't. But if there was, the government now—hah! And get the police to cooperate? Never. A few non-governmental organizations? Maybe. But if that's all, users can't be sure to be safe and wouldn't trust the NGOs. They'd stay hidden. They'd transmit. And the funding—who can sustain it? Nobody. USAID gives it for a while, then who knows. The Global Fund? Maybe. But only with strings attached. Kazakhstan won't like such strings. UNAIDS? Maybe yes, maybe no. So why bother writing the plan for action that I know is best? Everything is impossible. So I can't even start."

The whole class frowns in empathy.

Vinh says, "Viet Nam, too, we have the IDUs. Parents are ashamed of kids, they get high at the home. Government is very strong with morality, very anti-drug. Whole drug topic is taboo. You could never even say a word like *decriminalize*. But making jobs, giving hope to unhappy youth, educating parents—these are still possible." He grins. "Maybe."

Lena shrugs impatiently. "Jobs! Sure! We can give these discouraged, idle kids lots of jobs in the great post-Soviet economy!" She laughs with a bitter edge.

"But look, Lena," I say. "What's paralyzing you, this gap between what you know works in one place and a situation that prevents acting on it in another, *that's* actually what should be the focus of the paper. Instead of writing about 'Here's a good idea,' write about 'Here's a good idea, but it won't work.' The crisis *is* the subject. It's more interesting and more useful. You don't have to have the whole solution, the cure. That's not the point here. A well-reasoned analysis of obstacles and complexities that gets other people a little closer to an answer is good."

Lena exhales an audible sigh. "I don't have to solve the problem?"

"No. *You* don't have to solve the problem."

She sighs again. "You know, so much of my past writing has been for funding proposals, for NGOs at home. To seduce a funding source, any donor, I always have to sound so confident, appear certain that what I'm proposing will work. A lot of people get in the habit of writing that way. How else to get money? The RFP style makes everyone oversimplify, sound overconfident."

"So this isn't an RFP. For now you are still in the sheltered luxury of academia. Not that we want you to be up in the clouds, floating in abstraction. But you can afford to be thorough, to have insights, to weigh, explicitly, the reasons behind the difficulties."

"I don't have to come up with all the answers in this paper?"

A class chorus replies: "No!"

"But then who is my audience?" Lena looks very unhappy again. For a moment she hides her face in her beautifully manicured hands. "If I think of someone in government reading my insight, if I think of the guys who set policy reading my critique of the obstacles I tell them that they make themselves—I see myself unemployed. Maybe in prison." She laughs again. "So I am all stuck again. Paralyzed. Because you—" she flashes an insidious little smile at me, "*you* always tell us to remember the audience."

Now everybody laughs.

"Okay. So *now* imagine you have a friend in the Ministry of Health," I advise. "Someone—just one person could be enough, one person with a little courage—who would understand what you're saying, who's on good terms with the others and can translate your analysis into a language they understand."

"You know somebody like that?" asks Vinh.

Lena chews on the end of her pen, reflecting. "Maybe. Maybe Igor, who graduated from here last year." Now she smiles at me. "Okay. Let me try that. At least I don't have to have all the answers. Just knowing that helps."

"Next?" I ask. "Someone else?"

Everyone is quiet for a minute.

Finally Carmen breaks the silence. "I have a different paralysis problem. When I read the data set I have to work with, from the study of children who are heads of households in a community that has been devastated by AIDS in Uganda, my heart breaks."

Her heart breaks. The words tumble into our now deeper silence. Under my influence, words proliferate. Yet the bedrock of public health is the crushing, silent heartbreak we all once felt, that we almost never let ourselves feel or remember anymore. The heartbreak that made these students certain, once, that human beings could do better. That *they* could do better.

"How old are the children?" asks Fawzia.

"Maybe seventeen. Maybe ten. It depends. Even an eight-year-old will take charge, if he is the oldest. And if a grandmother or aunt does not step in."

"So what are you going to do with the data?" I ask.

"That's my problem. These kids alone, out of school, running in packs on the street sometimes, snorting glue, fending for themselves, lugging around the babies." Her voice catches. "I start crying. I can't write a word."

Vinh, who finds empathy so natural, perhaps even more natural than being the distinct self we insist he be in our American university, in our American life, and who slips so easily into everyone else's shoes, looks like he is ready to cry. Fawzia cups her hands over her eyes. Michael is doodling.

"Okay. Everybody's topic is depressing, right?" I say.

"Right," says Lena.

"If things were working fine, if kids were happy and healthy and well cared for, like kids should be, you would not be writing about this topic, right? If we really thought about it, I mean *really* thought about it, we could all sit here and cry and do nothing else, just weep over the suffering under every topic in the course."

They all frown at me, hoping I know where I'm going with this. I don't.

"So much *unnecessary* suffering, so much suffering caused by human greed and violence and indifference. Not to mention the earthquakes and droughts and cyclones and hurricanes. So many little *children* suffering." I think of Toby, the pudgy little boy in the courtroom, closed-mouth on the stand, facing the nervous man they all say is a murderer, a man who is his father no matter what he did—even a child of ten knows there's no going back, your father is your father—and an itch on the nose is an itch on the nose—and a small, high-pitched voice of panic begins to call out from my own insides. I ignore it. I am the teacher. "So much wealth, and yet where does it go?"

"Weapons of mass destruction."

"Luxury hotels."

"Militaries."

"Swiss bank accounts of ex-dictators."

"Huge gas-guzzling cars, mansions, vacation homes."

"Okay," I say. "So there's unspeakable excess among some sets of people, while others literally starve."

"It's always been like that," says Michael.

"Yup. So we pretend that when we must work under *resource constraints*, this is the natural order of things. Like it's built into the human condition. An indisputable given, non-negotiable. Some have, some do not. On the first day God created heaven and earth, and on the second he created disparities."

A few students laugh.

"That's the way it is. Even with so much waste and self-indulgence in our faces all the time. And we feel so helpless, so powerless. If we let ourselves."

"Oh God," says Carmen.

Lena lowers her head onto her hands on the table. Michael keeps doodling.

A sound like a whimper slithers out from someone, I can't tell who. I just hope it wasn't me. No, it wasn't; my own voice sallies forth in a deeper, croaking half-whisper. "Should we freewrite a little?" I need to buy myself some time.

"No!" The response is loud and vehement and unanimous.

"Okay." I pause. I sense I no longer have the inner resources to continue. I am a flubbering mass of jelly, barely contained, about to overflow my own boundaries. I want to put my head on the table and weep, too. And of course it is just then that Sam huffs and puffs his way through the door, coat slung over his arm, laptop in one hand, bulging briefcase in the other, two shirt buttons undone, pale abdominal flesh visible. Not even a tee shirt underneath. I check his fly. It's zipped. I am grateful for small mercies.

"Sorry I'm late," he mutters, panting. "Traffic on 93 was unbelievable." He looks around. "Christ, what's happened in here?"

Alice groans. "We got depressed over our topics."

"And we are so helpless," whines Carmen.

Vinh plants his hopeful gaze on me.

"No you're not." I struggle for words. "Your topics threaten to overwhelm you, but you are *not* helpless. That's why you went into public health. Your task, writing these papers, is not to have the *final* answer, but you do have to find at least a thread of positive action you can recommend. It's not just good *public* health, it's also good *mental* health, to seek out the opportunities, the small steps that we can advocate." I try hard to believe this myself as I am saying it.

"Here here," says Michael, limply and sarcastically.

"No, Erika is right," says Vinh. "Listen to what she says."

"Touchy-feely crap," Sam mumbles under his breath, opening his laptop as he plops into the seat next to me. "Can we just get on with the class?"

"We're getting there," I mutter back. "You could have helped with this pep talk, you know." His computer sings its little boot-up song. I see the screen light up. I take a big breath.

"Carmen, you will frame your data analysis in a way that informs policy on orphan care in Uganda. Your passion will translate, through clear and vivid writing, into an urgency that even the most jaded policy makers won't miss. Your presentation of salient anecdotes will reinforce the numbers and hold the readers' interest. They will see *children*, not only tables and percentages. Your active verbs with human actors will keep people in the forefront. The orphans will be subjects of sentences, not just passive recipients; they will refuse to be pushed semantically or syntactically to the margins. They will not simply be neglected, abused, infected, or taken out of school. *Someone* will be held responsible by your sentence structure: we will know *who* has neglected, infected, or abused them, *who* took them from school. Those accountable will not be able to hide behind the passive voice; they will have to be the subjects of their sentences, too."

"You go girl," says Marianne. All the students are now sitting up straight.

"Okay?"

"Okay," says Carmen. "Got it."

Everyone jots down notes, including Michael. Even *I* feel better. From the rubble and ashes, I could rise up.

"Oooh-kaay," says Vinh, as he scribbles feverishly.

Sam peers over the top of his glasses. "May we *begin* now?"

As I STROLL across the quad with my salad from the cafeteria in hand, skinny medical students stripped down to tee shirts run and leap in the new grass, tossing and catching Frisbees, eternal harbingers of spring in academia. Bodies seem to soar through the air. Sunlight soothes, even as a plane roars directly overhead, striving for altitude from a low take-off along its southerly inner-city flight path. A light breeze flutters the half-unfurled blossoms of a magnolia as the world pretends to be new and gentle again.

I feel stared at from behind and turn around quickly, expecting to see one of my students. But there are no students. The obese man, however, is following me from several yards away. Mr. Edwards limps a bit now; his waddle seems even slower than before, his ballooning torso slightly aslant. He is like a bigger-than-life-size inflated balloon, weighted at the bottom, listing from side to side. He wears a voluminous denim jacket, the cheap cloth too stiff, its blue overly bright. His hands are shoved into the pockets, which are ridiculously high for his long arms, making his bent elbows stick out awkwardly at his sides like handles of a poorly designed urn. He seems to be staring directly at me but shows no sign of noticing I've turned to face him. He squints, fending off glare. I stop at the grassy edge, turn my back to the sidewalk, and pretend to watch the airborne Frisbee ballet, holding my breath. Very slowly, he passes behind me. His gaze pierces my back like two long needles, but then he is past. When I start walking again, he is well ahead. I can keep an eye on *him* now. If his cowlick is shooting into the air, from this safe distance I can't see it.

I stop, sit on a wooden bench and open up my salad box as I watch Mr. Edwards come to a standstill just before he reaches the street at the eastern edge of the quad. He only stops for a second or two, then swivels on his heels and reverses direction, slowly limping back toward me on the same path. Maybe this is how he gets his exercise, doing laps back and forth through the quad between appointments or while he waits for his prescriptions to be filled. Wondering if he'll catch a glimpse of his son and if he does, refraining with all his might from approaching him. It is awkward, trying to toss my salad in the confines of a plastic box; the clot of brownish dressing adheres resolutely to the romaine and spinach leaves it first landed on, no matter where I push them. I push harder. A slice of tomato disintegrates under the pressure and a garbanzo bean hops into the lid and then onto the ground. I continue to wield the plastic fork uselessly among the leaves as the limping behemoth advances toward me and momentarily blocks out the sun as he passes. I steal a glance. He stops, takes his hands from his pockets and lowers his heavy bulk onto a bench at a diagonal across from mine, his arms first stretched straight out in front of him, then dropping as he rests the two hands on the broad mounds of his thighs. For nearly a minute he regards his sausage fingers intently, as if he had never noticed them before. He has lost more hair on top than I remember, his forehead recedes into half-baldness. But in back the thin gray hair grows long, too long, and hangs in a stringy fringe behind his ears and down his nape. He looks up, his face now blank and pasty, and settles his empty gaze on me. If this is Mr. Edwards, he is altered beyond recognition. Of course he would be, by now. (As I must be, too.) But then how can I be sure it is him? I close the plastic lid over my uneaten salad, lick dressing from the plastic fork and wrap the fork in a napkin. I peer at my watch, as if I am calculating, deciding something I suddenly remember needs to be decided. Without taking another peek at the bench diagonally across from me, I get up and walk quickly to my building.

IT IS A bad day.

First we discuss Blaise's topic, the value of offering voluntary HIV testing and counseling at workplace sites in Burundi.

"But are there any measurable outputs so far?"

These words issue from my own mouth, spoken across the seminar table to Blaise. His lips part, his bright eyes widen in the deep mahogany of his face, but he remains silent, giving me enough time to hear what I have just said. *Measurable outputs.* I have used the cursed words. The others are watching us and my face is burning, but still Blaise is silent. Is he dumbstruck because I have uttered these words, or because he is working on an answer?

"Ohmygod!" shrieks Alice. "Erika said *measurable outputs*! Her own pet peeve, let's see, pet peeve number"—Alice rummages through a pile of papers and pulls one page out—"pet peeve number four! On Erika's own list!" She smiles. "Right between using *impact* as a verb and *above-mentioned*."

"Off with her head," says Sam.

By this time I have buried my face in my hands. "I can't believe I said it. But I did. I heard myself say it. I am so ashamed."

Vinh says cheerfully, "This is the end of the world."

"Where are the lifeboats?" asks Fawzia. "Women and children first!"

I take my hands away from my face and try to regain a little of my authority. "What *is* an output?" I ask.

"Results," says Blaise.

"Products," says Alice.

"Data," says Vinh.

Marianne is thoughtful. "It depends on the situation. If you were talking about manufacturing, outputs might be computer chips. Or tee shirts. Or airplane parts."

"Or widgets," says Sam.

"What is widgets?" asks Fawzia.

"Never mind," says Sam.

I say, "All of these are good, precise words, you can almost see them, or hold them in your hand. Even the more abstract words like *results* or *products* are pretty good. So why would anyone use the word *output*?"

"Everybody uses that word," says Michael. "So what?"

"It's jargon," declares Fawzia, triumphant. "It only seems to mean something because everybody uses it."

"But even *you* used it," Michael accuses me.

"What did I really mean? What might we measure, in the case of Blaise's assertion that the uptake of counseling and testing was good after the educational campaign directed at factory women?" Oh God, I think: will they catch me on the word *uptake*, too?

"How many more women came for counseling and testing than before."

"How many started using condoms."

"How many more women went ahead and got treatment."

"How many more women and babies got AZT for the birth."

"Good. These are examples of relevant evidence. Evidence supports an argument; it logically develops a position. Outputs do nothing, except get put out. Inputs are even worse."

They laugh, but no sooner have I made this fumbling recovery from what I am certain is the slippery slope of my professional downfall, another blow strikes the class.

Lena says, "I have decided to change my topic."

Everyone groans.

"Finally I could not end my paralysis, knowing that the Kazakhstan government would never implement what I suggest to keep the injecting drug users safe. I tried to imagine a friend in the Ministry who would help, like Erika told me, so I thought of Igor. But after a paragraph or two, all I could see was Igor driving a nice new Mercedes car, wearing a Rolex watch; by the end of one page, I saw him in handmade Italian shoes and a fur coat, and me I saw in a freezing cold prison, shivering in little cotton uniform."

"That's a bit exaggerated, isn't it?" I ask.

Lena shrugs, frowning sullenly. "It's *imagination*. You said imagine, yes? So I imagined. And I never got any further than imagining."

"You gave up on drug users? Oh no," says Vinh, his sympathy oozing for Lena, for the drug injectors in her country, for drug injectors everywhere.

Fawzia smiles wryly, "So now you are writing about smallpox vaccination in Kazakhstan?"

We all laugh, happy that Fawzia, departing again today from her usual serious deadpan and very critical eye, would make such a good, apt joke and lighten things up. But Lena does *not* laugh; she sends Fawzia a surprised look. "How did you know?" Clearly Lena is not joking.

Many of us turn to Sam, who peers over the top of his glasses at his computer screen, grinning.

Lena soldiers on, tossing back the frizzy red corona of her hair. "Yes, I discussed with Sam. That is good, yes? He's our teacher. It seems best for me to write about a situation the government has not already failed."

We are all silent again.

"I will compare with Uzbekistan, another former Soviet country which is maybe already doing worse than us on bioterrorism preparation."

"Preparedness," mumbles Sam.

"Why pick a *worse* one to compare with?" I ask.

"Hey," says Alice, "this is really great!" She pokes a finger at Michael. "You've got Togo, I've got Ecuador, and now Lena has a couple of Stans. We'll have smallpox covered everywhere!"

"But there is no smallpox anywhere," says Fawzia.

After class, passing by my side of the seminar room quickly, Lena hovers like a hummingbird for just a second. "I know, I know,

I will have to take an incomplete and finish in the summer," she buzzes. Then she flutters out the door.

"WHAT KIND OF course is it," asks Nussbaum at a department meeting, "if half the students wind up taking incompletes?"

"What course is that?" asks Toby.

Sally doesn't seem to be following; she marks up a student assignment. Sam taps at his laptop keys. Rich doodles as he sneaks looks at a journal article. Horst is overtly worrying a text message on his cell phone. Bob looks blankly at the center of the table; I think he is asleep with eyes open again. Abby is writing in her schedule book. The rest of us try to appear attentive and engaged. Ben sashays in, fifteen minutes late, unapologetic.

Fiona looks sternly at Toby and says, "These kinds of issues do not have to be identified in public by name."

"Oh, so it's *your* course," smirks Toby. He has become truly despicable. No one has to be nice to him.

"It happens *not* to be my course, Toby," says Fiona.

"Maybe it's *my* course," says Ivan.

"Or mine," says Abby.

"Not half the students," I say. "Only three or four students out of twelve."

"So far," says Sam.

Fiona rolls her eyes. "It doesn't seem fair to talk about problems with specific courses in a full faculty meeting. Erika and Sam do *not* have to own this problem."

Nussbaum shrugs a mock-helpless shrug, grinning. "Hey, if the shoe fits . . ."

Twenty

❖

She was the one who used to write the not-quite sentimental stories.
Old-fashioned, even sweet. But now her stories have that edginess.
That edgy something . . . what do you call it? That edgy edge.

FAITH KNEELED ON a chair, pencil in hand, copying her English
vocabulary words, while her mother, weak now from sickness and
tired after a long day at the flower packing plant, stared blankly at
the page. It was the back-side of an advertising flyer and Faith had
placed it on the table right under the lightbulb dangling from the
ceiling. She had already drawn some lines on the paper with a ruler.
She tried to place words straight along the lines. Now she pressed
down with the pencil—but not too hard, not hard enough to break
the point—on the two long stems of a pair of *p*'s in *hippopotamus*,
which dipped below a line. Just as the *h* had stretched high above
it. Faith was almost eight years old. Her reading and writing were
good for her age. She said the word out loud, syllable by syllable.
From his favorite spot on the floor, Gilbert chirped in repetition,
"hip, hippo," and scooted a miniature truck back and forth and
around Monica's feet, despite its broken wheels.

"Po. Pa," said Faith, carefully separating the two syllables.

"Time for bed," yawned Monica.

"Ta," said Faith. "Mus." She gazed proudly at her handiwork, the complete word on paper. Then she began drawing, starting with a wide oval, followed by a rough rectangle in front.

Monica ran water from the tap into a pan, then set the pan on the primus stove. In Nairobi she had achieved a faucet with a fixed basin and drainpipe, a stove, a lightbulb. The children were clean. They were baptized and went to church. They went to school. Even the little one knew his alphabet.

"Do they have ears?" Faith asked. "Hippos?" She giggled. "Do hippos have ears? Do they hear?"

"Of course they do," said Monica. "Look at the picture in your book at school."

Faith drew small crescent ears on the rectangular head.

"Does God have ears?" Faith asked.

"Of course he does," said Monica.

"Have you seen them? Is there a picture in the book? How do I know for sure?"

Monica sighed. She remembered meeting up with Faith and another child on the path once as they came home from school, she remembered kissing Faith, then kissing the other little girl, the other child tugging at Monica's skirt urgently, declaring, "Faith said maybe there is no God. And teacher got *mad*!" And Faith said nothing about it, she just dropped the other little girl's hand and kept walking beside her. So Monica had said nothing about it. Ever. But now she said, "If God didn't have ears, how would he hear your prayers?"

Faith's eyes grew darker. "But he doesn't answer my prayers. So maybe he *doesn't* hear them."

Monica grasped Faith's hand in hers, pen and all. "Which prayers have not been answered?"

Faith bit down on her lip, looked at the floor, and refused to speak more.

Twenty-one

❖

One of them will snap first. Which one will it be?

RUSHING FROM THE bus stop one spring morning to get to a meeting on time, I see Nussbaum glide by in his Jaguar, which means today Lady N is out and about, ferrying the kids to ballet lessons and soccer practice and swim meets, in the family Hummer. At this last faculty meeting of the semester, he admonishes us: we need better customer service, more targeted marketing of our products for the students continuing into their second year. "Sell the summer courses hard. It's a simple matter of *positioning*. Push the *brand*, people."

"And let students know that the field practice opportunity in Indonesia is on sale," says Scott. "For a limited time only, we can send three students for the price of two."

Scott is the newest new guy, supposedly to help with the summer programs. He got the private office right away, with no stop in the harem. His last job was in marketing for a pharmaceutical company; he is not particularly tall or short, not noticeably thin or fat, and I'm pretty sure I don't know him or his father from Adam. Toby is unusually subdued today, leafing through a magazine and silent during the whole meeting.

Scott reports on the progress of renovations on a nearby building, referring to the upcoming move of our "headquarters." He has somehow become point man for logistics. Discussion intensifies about the new site, where there will be fewer private offices and, Scott informs us, a more collaborative atmosphere, consistent with what he calls our new organizational paradigm, facilitated by a cubicle structure.

"For *faculty*?" Fiona cries out in disbelief. "*Cubicles*? Dilbert goes to *grad school*?"

"Sarcasm is not helpful," says Nussbaum. His newly trimmed goatee seems especially animated today, hopping up and down as he speaks.

"What about private talks with students?" I ask.

"You will be able to reserve a conference room," says Scott.

"But every time I—or any faculty member—meet with a student, it's private—"

"You'll adapt to the innovation," says Nussbaum.

"But reading, writing, research, grading, the things faculty do, *by definition*, all require quiet concentration, privacy," says Fiona.

"Of course some people are more naturally inclined than others to cling to old paradigms and tired-out habits," Nussbaum replies.

Fiona and I exchange our arched-eyebrow, put-in-our-place glances. I lean forward and with both hands clench my fists on the table.

"What's that about?" whispers Ivan.

"I'm clinging to an old paradigm."

For nearly an hour Nussbaum and Scott hold forth on team networking around concept-driven properties, actionable management insights, knowledge exchange, primary and secondary target niches, internal clients, external vendors, the implementation of funder branding requirements, integration of online and offline marketing collateral, and the old reliable, ubiquitous deliverables. I have no idea what they're talking about. Are we still in a university, or has the paradigm already shifted completely? On the education superhighway, I am driving an Edsel uphill at thirty miles an hour, oblivious to the traffic that's desperate to pass as I watch for dirt roads and scenic turnouts.

"Hey," I whisper to Ivan. "How about bringing up something *real*? About *teaching*? You could get away with it. You're the only one who has the authority, the seniority." He also has the testosterone, which counts for Nussbaum.

At the end of the hour Nussbaum checks his watch, folds up his agenda, and tucks his PDA into his pocket. "Anything else?"

I angle my elbow into Ivan's rib. He clears his throat. "I wanted to revisit the issue of our instructional objectives as related to critical thinking." Good for Ivan. As if my Edsel wasn't bad enough, now he pulls in with his crank-up Model T.

"Was that on the agenda?" asks Nussbaum.

"Not precisely. But a few months ago we talked about introducing a staged, progressive development of students' critical thinking skills coordinated through our core courses and across the electives and then the thesis."

"It was a really good idea," says Fiona.

Ivan continues. "I expected in the natural follow-up that we would have returned to the topic by now."

Nussbaum rolls his eyes. "Now? Here?"

"It's a faculty meeting," Ivan chuckles hoarsely. "When else would the faculty discuss the department's teaching mission?"

Scott sniggers audibly, perched on the edge of his chair, tapping his foot.

Sam's cell phone rings and he answers it right here at the meeting table. "Yes? No, it's done. No, no, I'll take it now." He rushes out of the room and continues shouting into his phone within earshot. "But the contractor won't be finished until Friday! *Friday!*"

Ivan persists. "The students' approach to research these days is terribly immature and I'm not sure if we are doing enough to stop this view of knowledge as mere facts, Google-able facts, a commodity—packaged, static, utilitarian."

"Google-able, I like that," says Horst. He leans sideways and says to Abby in an only slightly lowered voice, "It was a great show on Broadway. Did you catch it? *Les Googlables.*" His French accent is perfect.

"Spoon-fed with PowerPoint presentations," says Ivan.

"Friday at five!" shouts Sam from the hallway.

"Les Googs," Abby whispers loudly, then snorts back laughter.

Ivan raises his voice. "Like the burgeoning problem with plagiarism—the phenomena are not unconnected—learning, knowledge have been—" He falters, grasping for words, derailed from his usual effortless oratory by the unfamiliarity of his own loudness—"devalued, commodified—like, uh, health itself has been commodified, some would say—" As he hems and haws and repeats himself, what little attention remains in the room palpably drops away. Even Fiona has begun to fidget, curling and uncurling the corner of a page. But he goes on. "I'm worried . . . concerned about—is this inevitable? I don't think so—the devaluation, the commodification of what used to be an educational *process* that we as faculty once *modeled* and *fostered* and—"

"Yada, yada, yada," Nussbaum cuts in. "If it's so important, get it on the agenda for the next meeting, all right?" A groaning chorus of our chairs scuffing back along old parquet rules out further discussion.

On the way out I squeeze Ivan's hand. "You tried. You did good. You get credit for trying."

"Oh shut up," he replies.

"THERE'S ANGEL FOOD cake." Toby grins in my doorway, but it's Tina, I think, who woos me with low-fat treats now; Tina as much as Toby is trying to win me over, to ensnare me in their family goo. "And fresh strawberries."

"I have class in just a few minutes, Toby."

"Okay, so have it when you get back from class. If there's any left. No, wait. I'll put aside a plate for you."

"No thanks, that's okay."

"I will," he says adamantly. "Tina made it herself, y'know. I *will* cut a piece of cake and put it aside for you, with some of the strawberries, so you can have it when you come back."

Silent, I staple together a packet of handouts for class.

"She didn't make the berries herself," says Toby.

I continue to collate and staple.

"That's a joke," he says. He laughs. "Of course she couldn't actually make strawberries. Even if we had a garden, which we don't."

I hit the stapler especially hard on the last packet.

"Anyway, you'd say she *grew* the strawberries, or she *picked* the strawberries, not she *made* the strawberries, right?" He grins. "I mean, you're the writing person. The *word* person. Nobody can *make* strawberries."

I push the packets together into a sloppy pile and glance up at Toby. "What is it today, Toby?"

He waits a few seconds, then clears his throat. "I decided not to go to Kenya."

"*You* decided? Yourself?"

"Yup. Well, I decided and then I talked it over with Tina and Tina thought it was better this way, too."

"What does Nussbaum say?"

"He's disappointed. He knew I would bring the necessary managerial skill set. I would have been his real right-hand man on the ground. But he understands. He says he understands, and I think he really does understand."

"*What* does he understand?"

"My family responsibilities. One baby, another on the way. Tina's still in the first trimester and not feeling so great. Morning sickness, y'know? It's not the optimum time for us, for me to spend weeks in Africa. From the family point of view, I can't justify that kind of trip now. Hopefully this will not be a big setback for my career and I'll be able to maximize future opportunities."

I say, "And the little children in Kenya? Don't they still need you?"

He sighs. "Frances says they're okay. I'm not convinced, but I'm hoping if I keep reminding her, she'll stay on top of what's going on there. It is her job, after all."

I gather up my folder of notes, my overhead transparencies and handouts for class and stand up. "You would have been in way over your head."

"I figured you'd be happy I'm not going," says Toby.

I shrug. "Not happy. Relieved." I switch off my lamp and the overhead light. Toby backs away and moves aside as I exit, close the door and lock up.

"I'll save you a piece of cake and some strawberries," he calls after me as I race down the stairs.

IVAN IS PACKING again, this time for a conference in Bangkok. I look out his bedroom window, mesmerized by rainwater dripping from the broken gutters of the house next door. He touches my shoulder to get my attention, then holds out his toiletries case. "Do you want to check it for contraband?"

"Not really."

"You sure?" He frowns a cute puppy-dog frown, a thick lock of hair falling into his eyes. He really should have a haircut before he goes and does his public speaking halfway around the world, but I don't remind him.

He pushes the toiletries case into my hands. Does he want me to see that he packed condoms again or that he *hasn't* packed condoms again? That the same condoms from the last trip are still there, untouched? Or that only one remains?

I open the case. Right on top are two box cutters, blades extended. "Very funny." I take them out, close them, put them on the dresser. He grins. Then I go straight for the compartment with the packets of stain remover and insect repellent. And condoms. Yes, they are there. The same ones? Fewer? More? Who knows. I take one out. He pushes up his lower lip and blows the lock of hair out of his eyes but it only flutters a little and falls back. Looking at me without a frown or a smile, his face has shed its endearing mask. He is simply there, himself, a little worried, a little tired, turning sixty. And seventy. And eighty. Maybe even ninety. I like him best this way.

I move closer, circle his middle with both my arms, gently push him against the wall and then unbuckle and unzip him so fast, he puts up no resistance, he is instantly aroused. I am out of my clothes in no time and have the condom on him in no time, in just one try. And then I am on him, too, we swivel around, separating only a few seconds so he is sitting on the bed and I am sitting facing him and we are bound together again and we rock each other back and forth, wordless. We are lost in each other and nobody is too small. Nobody has a fugue. Nobody talks, not even at daybreak when I leave. And this we both know without a word is the last time.

"THERE'S APPLE PIE." That is what I think I hear, but when I look up from my desk I know I'm mistaken.

"I beg your pardon?"

"There's a problem. Hi." Nussbaum hovers in my doorway, unusually early in the day, strumming at his little beard. "Toby's gone missing on his way to Kenya. Frances went to meet him yesterday but he never came through the customs and immigration line at the airport in Nairobi. Tina's pretty sure he got on the first plane, to Amsterdam, though of course she couldn't go past the security check-in with him. But she saw him off. We're trying to get the passenger verification for both planes. He may have gone AWOL in Amsterdam, though he had plenty of time to make the connecting flight."

"Maybe he's asleep on one of the reclining chairs in the upstairs lounge at Schiphol. They're pretty comfortable."

"This is no time for jokes." Nussbaum scowls.

"I thought he *wasn't* going to Kenya."

"He talks to you, yes? People see him talking to you."

People. Which of Nussbaum's spies tiptoes by my office in the early mornings, keeping track? "He stops by sometimes in the morning to tell me there's coffee."

"Did he say anything that might make you think something was amiss?"

"He told me he *wasn't* going to Kenya."

Nussbaum doesn't seem to hear what I've said. "Tina thought you might know something."

"Why would she think *I* know something?"

"Because he talks to you. Because he must tell her that he talks to you."

"*Everyone* talks to me. I don't remember. All he told me was that he was staying here, that he *would not* travel now because of family responsibilities. Which he said you understood."

"What exactly did he say I understood?"

"That it was better for him not to travel right now because of the kid and the baby on the way and Tina's morning sickness."

Nussbaum looks at the floor. "There's a baby on the way?"

Why am I so happy to see him caught by surprise? Shame on me. "I haven't personally seen any lab results. Toby's family is none of my business." Now if that isn't the most outlandish thing I've said in ages, what is? "But Toby told me Tina was pregnant, and he told me you had accepted his decision not to go."

Nussbaum swats the doorjamb with the flat of his hand. "Shit." He swings around and looks down the hall, as if expecting someone to appear and put him back in control, his own rescue deus ex machina. But of course no one appears; no one is ever here this early except me and Toby. "Shit," he says to the empty hall. I love it. Then he turns and faces me again. "I had him booked on a nonrefundable flight to Nairobi. That's what *I* had."

"I would not worry about the cost of the ticket before I knew if Toby was alive and well."

He scowls. "You think you know somebody. You think you can *trust* somebody." Nussbaum pounds on the door with a fist now. "Shit!" He pounds his fist again. "The *liar*."

"Maybe you ought to ask Tina about the baby." Maybe you sent an ax murderer to Kenya.

He scowls more.

I say, "Just because someone always makes a point of saying exactly what you want to hear doesn't mean you know him. Or that you can trust him. Often it means just the reverse." These things are self-evident, common knowledge. You would not even need a citation.

He glowers at me. I hold back a smile, a belly laugh, a dance.

THE RINGING PHONE wakes me from a sound sleep. The clock says
4:25. I am groggy and annoyed when I grope, pick up, and hoarsely
mumble hello. The line is silent, except for a slight echo-y vacancy,
a distant almost-hum. "Hello?" I say again.

"There's cocoa and croissants," says a hoarse voice back.

"Who is this?"

"There's windmills. There's daffodils. There's whippoorwills."
Toby laughs.

"You're still in Amsterdam? Why are you in Amsterdam?
Everybody's worried about you."

Silence again.

"What's going on Toby?"

He replies with mimicry. "What's going on Toby?"

"Are you drunk? What time is it there? Why are you there?"

Again he echoes. "Are you drunk? What time is it there? Why
are you there?"

"Toby, please. Where are you?"

"Toby please," he mimics. "Where are you?"

I wait. What I hear then, I think, is a sniffle. Then another.
Perhaps it's an itch on the tip of his nose. The little boy on the stand
now stares at *me*.

"Toby?"

Silence is his answer.

I am just about to rest the receiver down in its cradle, but I bring
it back. "Toby?" Now I hear only the vaguest faraway static. "I
knew your dad, Toby. A long time ago. He was my biology teacher
in high school. I followed his story, later. I know what happened to
him. I know what happened to you."

I hear something like a catch in a throat, almost a hiccup. He may still be on the line. Or he may not be, he might not have been there for a while. Maybe it was just an electronic blip. A transatlantic sound glitch.

"Toby?"

Silence.

"Toby? I'm sorry, Toby. I really am. Please come home. It's okay. Really. I've never told anyone. I never *will* tell anyone. It's okay. Really. Call Tina now. Call Nussbaum. Come home, Toby."

Now the silence is complete: no hiccup, no hum, no static, no echo. But maybe, after a while, comes a very quiet click.

I hang up.

"IT'S A HIPPOPOTAMUS."

"Another one?" Monica whispered, her breath labored and raspy.

Faith giggled. "A happy hippo," she said in English. "I hope."

The very last time Faith visited her mother, in a crowded hospital ward in Nairobi, not knowing it was the final visit, not connecting the way her mother had become with the way her father had once been (she was only eleven, after all), not even suspecting that the move to Auntie Mary's house would last more than a day or two, she brought Monica her ninth drawing of a hippopotamus, her best by far. But Monica could not really see it. Her eyes were now puffed slits receding in their hollows, filmy. She could not discern the outlandishly big, heavily lobed ears Faith had drawn on the hippo, or the looped rings in those ears onto which Faith had so painstakingly glued tiny flecks of gold glitter (scraped off a holiday project at school). She patted the paper with her hand, smiled, and weakly felt her way from the paper beside her on the cot up Faith's arm and shoulder and neck to Faith's cheek. Faith held Monica's hot hand against her face for a few minutes. It burned her cheek, but Faith kept it there. And Monica kept it there, with Faith's slender fingers entwined with hers. Their fingers were nearly the same size now, Monica's so shrunken and Faith's still growing. But Mary, impatient, yanked at Faith's other hand. "Time to go," she said. Embarrassed in this cavern of sickness, Mary said good-bye to Monica like it was any old good-bye of any old day to anybody at all. As the woman and the child stepped away, maneuvering between so many cots while avoiding each set of sunken eyes, the sheet of paper fluttered off Monica's blanket to the floor. Nobody noticed. Soon it was stepped on by a shuffling old woman carrying a basket of roasted yams and *ugali* for a niece a few beds away. With the very first dragging footstep, the glitter was gone. With a few more, the piece of paper creased again and again into a smudgy accordion. And then the remains of the trampled page got stuck to the bottom of the left shoe of the ward's only nurse that evening, giving her the faintest, virtually unconscious sense of lumpy irritation for several hours of her tireless but doomed efforts until finally, waiting for the *matatu* home, she scraped her heel back and forth on the edge of a rock beside the roadway.

Twenty-two

❖

She woke up in a foreign country. The foreign country she woke up in was her life.

THE LAST DAY of classes, I take my sandwich outside and find a bench. Of course the sky is perfectly blue, crisscrossed directly overhead by broad contrails, like streaks laid on with wide white chalk. Young men and women in blue scrubs sit in the shade at picnic tables, while clusters of students and workers sprawl on the grass or sun themselves on benches. White coats march past, stethoscopes looping out of pockets. Three hygienists from the dental school in matching floral-print smocks eat salads on the bench across from me. A steady parade ambles along between us. Several of my own students greet me and chat for a few seconds. Then they go away. Fiona dashes by, late for a meeting, and then Ben passes in a sprint, even later for his class.

Before long I spot the heavyset man slowly limping toward me, his peculiar swaying gait more pronounced than usual today. From this perspective I see that his shoulders, though rounded, are actually quite narrow, but his midsection balloons into a perfect sphere, as if he had been inflated with an air pump. The three hygienists suddenly get up in unison from the bench across from me, a bench wide enough to accommodate the whole expanse of Mr. Edwards. The hygienists saunter back toward the dental school. I hold my breath as if one less respiration, one fewer disturbance of the atmosphere, however infinitesimal the difference it may make in the composition and alignment of the campus universe, might still somehow alter the man's trajectory and prevent him from noticing this sudden opening, this perfectly timed invitation *for him* to rest.

But no, no such luck. He stops, swivels to face me. Arms outstretched in front of him, he lowers himself onto the bench, then rests a hand, stubby fingers splayed, on the broad cushion of each thigh. He rocks back and forth for a few seconds, settling in place, then lifts his chin, closes his eyes, smiles, and offers his round face and shiny pate to the sun, his stringy gray fringe, longer than ever, creeping down his neck and shoulders.

I observe his doughy face for a while; it doesn't move. A backpack-saddled student stops between us, talking on her cell phone. When she folds it up and moves on, I squeeze a very small piece of bread from my sandwich into a spitball and lob it across the path. It bounces right off Mr. Edwards's wide forehead. His eyes remain closed, his smile unchanged. I pull off another small piece of bread, press it into another tiny rounded missile and, after more walkers have gone by, flick it across. I don't know why I'm doing this. *This* is really bad behavior. The spitball misses completely. I wait while an eminent pair of gray-haired doctors passes, deep in conversation. Then a delivery guy rattles by with huge jugs of spring water balanced on a narrow, wobbly dolly. On my third try, with a piece of crust kneaded in, the tiny bullet strikes the flat of his cheek and stays there for a second or two. He shakes it off, opens his eyes, sits up, squints, looks left and then right, then glares straight at me. I stare back.

"Your son went missing," I say.

"What son?"

"Toby. After we get him back from the hospital in Amsterdam, they'll send him to a classier place than the one you're in."

"Huh?" He laughs a squeaky, high-pitched laugh.

"I tried to talk to him, but he wouldn't talk to me. Neither will Tina."

"Lady, what's your problem?" He gives me a very beady look. I finish my sandwich. I take my time.

Then I say, "Have *you* ever talked to Toby since you got out of prison? You should, you know. You should talk to him. He never understood. That violence seemed to come from out of nowhere. But it always comes from somewhere, doesn't it?"

He screws up his face. "Huh? What the fuckin' fuck are you talking about?" He stares at me, mouth open, starting to laugh again. "Holy shit, you're even crazier than I am." With some difficulty, he rises to his feet. "Hey, lady!" His voice gets louder and squeakier as he takes a step toward me, and I cower, I shrink back and flinch, my hands jerking up to shield my face. But he laughs. Was he laughing when he pulled out the ax? "What fuckin' floor did *you* come off of? Fifth? Fourth? No, I bet it was fifth. They let you *off* that floor? Or did you *escape*? Holy shit, man." He squeaks again, even higher pitched. Did he squeak when he cut her into pieces? Did he squeak when he shoved the body parts into Dumpsters?

He turns away from me, muttering and laughing. "Holy fuckin' shit," he declares loudly. People around us stare at him. A few send me sympathetic glances as I sit up straight again. Everyone on the sidewalk, even those behind, gives him an extra-wide berth as he hobbles away, swaying rhythmically to one side and then the other, a lumbering, whacked-out metronome.

THOUGH NUSSBAUM WILL likely do a bed check later on in the afternoon, hell-bent that we worker bees never slip out early on *his* watch, I do not go back to my office or tell anyone where I am. I vanish into the campus foot traffic, among the suits, white coats, scrubs, jeans, backpacks, stethoscopes, cell phones. I walk. I walk past campus lunchtime into real life. After the gainfully occupied have retreated back into their offices and classrooms, the vast Boston marginalia—the humble, the outcast, the bleeding and wounded—are left on the street, at bus stops, on buses, and park benches. In front of me, a Vietnamese woman I often see pulls her shopping cart full of goodies scavenged from upscale trash, bumping hard along the new faux-antique brick sidewalk toward a makeshift Friday flea market that straggles on Tremont Street. I don't follow her all the way, but jump onto a bus heading downtown. At the next stop, a man staggers on and reels to the midsection of the bus, cursing loudly; he gestures to a woman across the aisle from me to take her stuff off the seat beside her, as well she should. As he sits, he berates her under his breath with coarse, slurred words; I can make out only *selfish bitch, worthless junk*. Stone-faced, she works at balancing her bags on her lap, works at making herself invisible, uncursable. He mutters awhile, then quiets down and begins to swig from an unhidden bottle of rum. A West Indian proselytizer with the joy of Christ's forgiveness in his voice has been loudly exhorting and leafleting the back of the bus. Now he comes forward, singles out the drinker, and tells him he would like to save his particular endangered soul. As his patter, ringing with certitude, becomes more personal and precise, honing in on the demon in the bottle, the mutterer becomes more belligerent and berates the smiling missionary, too. "Fuck you, I don't want your salvation, get the hell outta my face." Clutching her bags, the woman next to him keeps staring stonily straight ahead, offended and scared and striving toward invisibility but damned if she'll give up the seat. Across from the Super 88 Chinese grocery, a burly, surly looking man gets on wearing a large stuffed backpack; clambering past me, he knocks me hard with the pack. At this off-hour, the atmosphere on Boston's few-and-far-between buses feels tougher, more hostile than at the better-traveled, middle-class hours, a simmering cauldron of anger and impatience and resentment. Here, people squeezed to the bottom of Boston's chilly social waters take their rancor out on one another. In front of me, blocking the middle door, two teenage girls with fat, expressionless babies jabber on their phones, oblivious to the babies or the passengers who, with each lurch of the bus, get walloped by unrestrained strollers. And we. Do lurch. The driver stops short and starts with jerks because she's just as pissed as everybody else, maybe more. When the burly surly man with the backpack wants to get out at Temple Street where I am getting out, where nearly everyone is getting out, he tries to push past me and stomps on my sandaled foot; I hear myself bark, "Just *wait*!" He waits.

At Downtown Crossing, before schools let out and kids clog the streets, down-and-out men with long, unkempt beards wander and slink between the knots of blue-eyed tourists who are following the Freedom Trail. These men look undernourished and stunned, shell-shocked not so much by their old wars but by this urban life with no foothold for them; I pass several in just a few minutes, and they all seem to me to be the same man, one universal homeless veteran from the veterans' shelter nearby. Where is the statue, the monument to *him*? Where is *his* stop on the Freedom Trail? A woman with a slim waist set like a stem into a squat bulging tomato of an ass in tight red pants helps guide a wild-dreadlocked guy in a wheelchair—they weave from side to side, blocking the way of two elderly Japanese sightseers coming toward them, making it treacherous for me to try to pass them from behind. But still I walk and walk.

At what's left of Haymarket, beside the boondoggled wasteland of the Big Dig, I enter a muted hullabaloo, the tinny hum and holler of the nickel-and-dimed. This is not Place d'Aligre on a raucous Sunday morning or Rue Mouffetard, but it will do. People shop amid tired lettuces, crates of mangoes, boxes of overripe berries, skeins of scallions, oceans of onions, heaps of yams and patatas and manioc, tubers I've never seen before, cantaloupes gone soft or cantaloupes so green and hard they will never ripen, slabs of fish with scales intact, ropes of squid, deceivingly appetizing hunks of cheese that are either tasteless or expiring in inedible molds, and whatever other surplus from wholesale markets it takes for destitute families to scrape by in this gilded city in this gilded age. Total gridlock in the narrow passageway sets off a chain reaction of shouting and pushing. Where people's carts and totebags block the route, I, too, push and squeeze through.

"Five for a dollar, bud. Take it or leave it."

"I give you one dollar for seven."

"Forget it! I'm already losing as it is. Nothing's ever cheap enough for you people."

"Six then."

"Does this guy understand English? Five!"

The languages and smells and bargaining rhythms diluted from the marketplaces of every continent, of every island in the Caribbean and province of China, converge in these two or three cramped blocks of stalls. In the swirl of clothes are flowing batiks, *jalabiyas* and saris, embroidered *kufis* and chiffon *hijabs*. South Asian men in *salwar kameez* and Somali women in colorful head-dress, long, printed cotton skirts, and acrylic sweaters pick through potatoes beside stout wooly Russian couples, turbaned Sikhs, young Bosnians in blue jeans, wary Haitians in bright tropical shirts. Latin Americans from a dozen different countries, with and without pa-pers, keep a low profile. Chili peppers of every variety sell fast.

"Take your hands off!" shout the vendors who insist on filling bags themselves, reaching under the layer of large, fresh-looking produce to mix in the pock-marked seconds, the runts, the squished, the rotted, the leaves gone yellow.

"Gimme those big ones over there."

"Okay, honey, for you I'll do that. What else?"

In loud Chinese, two short women chat with each other over wilted cilantro and limp snow peas at a stall where the ignoramus of a vendor at the same time singsongs a mockery of Chinese speech right in their oblivious faces. I am shocked. I send him a murderous glare. "That's a good way to lose business," I say.

"Listen lady, for every one like you or them, I got a hundred loyal customers." He resumes his deliberately insulting, pretend Chinese.

In all the years, always at my desk or in my classroom, I never before took the bus or subway to Haymarket on a Friday; never saw people getting on with their empty shopping bags and carts; never saw them struggling with the weight of their bounty going back. I keep walking. Nonstop demolition and construction occupy the financial district like a foreign army, with streets torn up for gas-line repairs and sidewalk replacements; jackhammers rumble and drill at full throttle, cement mixers churn, pile drivers pound. Grating noise and bone-shaking noise and headache-making noise bombard from every direction, not just around the sprawling Big Dig sites but wherever I walk. Concrete is drilled and shattered into pieces and hauled away all over town, piles of debris rise, piles of construction material shrink. Sidewalks are closed off helter-skelter; sloppy chain-link fencing and plywood pieces piled overhead offer pedestrians narrow passage in the margins of roadways, the illusion of protection from debris falling from above or traffic slamming from beside. Over the sidewalks loom scaffolding, cranes, wrecking balls. Enraged drivers accelerate as pedestrians try to finish crossing. A woman rolls down her window and shouts to a driver in the lane beside her, "Why the fuck don't you learn to drive before you get on the road?" She rolls the window back up. On State Street I dodge a series of briskly walking, well-dressed men and women on cell phones who fail to notice who's around them and stop for nothing;

I freeze as bicycles surprise me from behind, whizzing past against the light, and then I make room for slick investment bankers, aspiring rappers in voluminous jeans, administrative aides in straight skirts and sneakers, all lost in the faraway world of their iPod earbuds. Shared public space no longer exists. On Court Street or Milk Street, in Post Office Square, even across the windswept desert of City Hall Plaza, the nonstop, driven workday's accumulations and privatizations and gentrifications feel as hostile and rancorous as the mood among the weary and downtrodden on the buses.

This is Boston's march of progress. These are our times.

Twenty-three

❖

They undress, men in one cavernous room, women in another. Hundreds
of them throw their clothes into clear plastic bags. The guards pretend
not to look at the people's nakedness and the people pretend not to look
at the guards'. They spray us with something foul smelling, then order
us to get into the regulation tunics and loose pants, which are made
of soft unbleached gray paper, a texture like paper towels. The baggy
tunic pulls on right over my head; the pants close snugly with velcro in
front. We get back in line. "For the gas chambers?" I ask the woman
behind me. She laughs, her face filled with scorn. "No, for the plane."
The guards pat us down one more time. "The people go on one flight,
the baggage and clothes and every bit of stuff on another," says Safiya,
who turns out to be ahead of me in line wearing a gray paper burka. I
recognize her eyes twinkling through the narrow opening. "That's the
way it is now," she says. I realize my books are gone, my snacks for
the trip, my extra shoes, everything. "But I don't have my boarding
pass anymore," I whimper. Now a crowd of women laughs. "Look at
your shirt. It is printed on your shirt," says a young woman with a
heavy accent I can't place. I glance down at my chest and sure enough,
the paper tunic says FLIGHT #911, big as life. It has my name on it.
How could we not have known? "Hurry," says Safiya. "It's waiting
for us on the runway." "You're coming, too?" I marvel. "I'm so glad."
Hand-in-hand and unhindered by our loose, fluttery paper covering,
we run fast, our feet barely touching the warm tarmac.